I heard someone pick up and Roy took the phone. He was still holding tight to the front of my jacket with one huge fist.

"Mr. Khachadurian? This is Roy from the club. Yes. I'm with John Blake, he says you— Yes, in his apartment. Wayne did. Because he's sticking his nose— He's hanging around the club, he's bothering the girls— No, I haven't. Yes. Yes. Yes, I understand." He slammed the phone down.

He pulled me close again. "You're one lucky son of a bitch," he said. He shoved me back and my knees buckled against the bed. I went sprawling. Then he was standing above me, blocking what little light came in through the window. I didn't see his fist come down, but I felt it as he buried it deep in my belly.

"Murco," I croaked.

"I don't work for Murco," he hissed. "I work for Wayne Lenz." An uppercut slammed against the underside of my chin, snapping my head back against the mattress. "That's first of all. Second, I don't like getting sprayed in the eyes." One more punch, this one aimed at my groin. I turned and caught it on my hip.

"He'll kill... he'll kill you." I could barely get the words out.

"Well, now, that's third," he said, and I could hear the satisfaction in his voice. "The man said don't do any permanent damage. Didn't say don't hit you." The next blow caught me in the side of the head. After that, I didn't feel the rest, just heard them as they landed...

Little Girl
LOST

by Richard Aleas

A HARD CASE CRIME NOVEL

A HARD CASE CRIME BOOK
(HCC-004)
October 2004

Published by

Dorchester Publishing Co., Inc.
200 Madison Avenue
New York, NY 10016

in collaboration with Winterfall LLC

ISBN 0-8439-5351-9

The name "Hard Case Crime" and the Hard Case Crime logo
are trademarks of Winterfall LLC. Hard Case Crime Books are
selected and edited by Charles Ardai.

Printed in the United States of America

Visit us on the web at www.HardCaseCrime.com

For Naomi

LITTLE GIRL LOST

Chapter 1

The headline made me sit down when I read it, that and the picture next to it and the article that spilled out over two columns underneath.

After I finished, I spread the paper out on the table, flattened it down with both hands, and stared at the photo. I wasn't reading, not any more, just watching the girl in the photo stare back at me, a big smile on her face, all her teeth showing, her eyes squinting against the photographer's flash, blond bangs hanging down under the peak of her mortarboard cap. That was one of two photos the paper had run; the other was on page nineteen, where the article continued. I didn't turn to page nineteen, not again, just stood up, bearing down on the table, leaning on my fists, and looked at her. The strangest thought came to me then: I thought about the bird.

It was made of styrofoam, with a yellow-and-red coating on it meant to look like feathers, a black plastic beak, and wire feet twisted into claws at the ends. I found it in the incinerator room at the end of the hall, in a balsa wood cage balanced on the rim of the slop sink. I'd come out to throw out the kitchen garbage for my mother, so I went ahead and dragged the door to the incinerator open and let the knotted plastic bag slide down the chute. But my eyes were on the bird, the shoddy styrofoam bird in its shoddy wooden cage.

One of our neighbors must have thrown it out, either the Tolberts or the Nelsons or Mrs. Knechtel in 14-D. No one would mind if I took it. My mother complained that it was filthy, but it wasn't, not very, and when I promised to wash it off, she said she'd let me keep it.

My father put a hook in the side of my bookcase and hung the cage on it, higher up than I could reach, and it stayed there, where I could see it every time I lay in bed, for the next ten years. My father left us somewhere along the way, but the bird stayed.

When Miranda Sugarman finally let me sleep with her, she did it looking up at that bird, a ten-year accumulation of dust mottling its coat, the cage splitting where the hook bit into the wood. It was the night before we graduated from high school and only a week before she would leave New York for summer school in Los Alamos, where she hoped to get a head start on the pre-med courses that would put her on track for a career as an optometrist, or an ophthalmologist, I could never remember which.

But that night I remember. I remember her eyelids trembling as she kissed me and how, afterwards, she weaved her fingers into my hair and pulled my head to her chest. I remember the curve of her shoulders as she leaned over the side of the bed to pick her glasses up off the floor. I remember listening to her heart as it hammered slower and slower against her ribs. Her chest was sticky with perspiration and so was my cheek, and we lay like that for a long time.

Out of nowhere she said, "I hate that thing. That bird. I really do."

I followed her glance and it was as though I were noticing the cage up there for the first time. It was an ugly, god-awful thing. I couldn't remember why I'd ever wanted it. I stood on tiptoe to get it down, wobbling a little as blood rushed to my head. Miranda laughed and I felt her hands around my waist, trying to hold me back, but I carried the cage out to the living room and she fol-

lowed, my blanket wound around her body. She hissed at
me as I unlocked the front door—"You're naked!"—but
she held the door for me and I walked out into the hall,
past 14-B and 14-C and 14-D. The door to the incinerator room squeaked as I opened it and again, once I'd put
the cage on the edge of the sink, when I let it slam shut.

I walked back, all the length of that long hall, to where
Miranda waited wrapped in my blanket, a look of mis-
chief and delight shining in her face; and at the last
instant, while a neighbor might still have opened the
door and seen her, she opened the blanket and let it fall
to her feet.

A sign of things to come? I didn't see it that way then.
I only knew, in that instant, and maybe only for that
instant, that I loved her: loved her as only an eighteen-
year-old escaping from virginity and high school in the
same night can. We swept the blanket under us. It didn't
matter to us that we were in my mother's living room. We
struggled to be silent, and failed. Thankfully, my mother
didn't wake up—or, if she did, she was discreet enough to
stay in her bedroom with the door closed. Or if she
wasn't, we never noticed.

The following afternoon, as I mounted the stage to the
sound of our music teacher pounding out "Pomp and
Circumstance" on the piano, I was struck by a thought.
Last night, I'd left the bird in exactly the same place I'd
found it ten years earlier, in more or less the same position on the edge of the sink. And despite the decade that
had passed, we still had all the same neighbors. One of
them was the person who had thrown the thing out in the
first place. What a shock it would be, I thought, what a
Twilight Zone kick in the head, if the same neighbor who
had thrown the bird out all those years earlier happened
to walk into the incinerator room today and see it there,

exactly as he or she had left it ten years ago. What would it be like? To think that you have safely disposed of something, that for better or worse it is out of your life forever, and then to walk into a room ten years later and find it there again, staring you in the face?

I saw Miranda for the last time a week later. She went away, and despite the best intentions on both sides we didn't stay in touch. I didn't know what happened next in her life, but I could imagine: after college, she settled down into a safe, sensible, hard-working Midwestern life, turned into a damn good doctor, while I—I stayed in New York and turned into what New York turns people into.

That was where I thought the story ended. And it was—until I walked into a room ten years after our graduation and saw Miranda Sugarman's yearbook photo staring at me out of the *Daily News* under a headline that said "Stripper Murdered."

Chapte r 2

Visiting a strip club in the middle of the day is like visiting a well-lit haunted house. The magic, such as it is, is gone. At night, the Sin Factory was probably decked out like a casino, with a flashing marquee and a tuxedoed bouncer checking IDs at the door. Maybe even a velvet rope to make the patrons feel special when they were let in. But at three in the afternoon there was no one at the door, the neon was turned off, and even the beat of the music leaking out into the street sounded sluggish and half-hearted.

Under glass in a frame on the door were photos of this week's featured performers, Mandy Mountains and Rachel Firestone. In her photo, Mandy was cradling breasts some mad doctor had built for her out of equal measures of silicone and cruelty. Rachel's photo showed a thin brunette straddling a chair backwards, her bare breasts peeking out between the slats. Judging by their shape, hers had gone under the knife as well, but next to Mandy's, Rachel's breasts looked almost modest. Either to keep the cops from complaining or to keep passers-by from getting too much of the show for free, management had stuck tiny silver stars over each woman's nipples. Along the top of the frame, a printed card announced the dates on which each woman would be appearing. Rachel had more than a week left, but tonight was Mandy's last night.

I pulled the door open. The place was smaller than most strip clubs I'd seen, just a single, narrow room with a bar against one wall and a tiny wooden stage at the far end. Mirrors on all the walls struggled to make the place and the crowd it held seem larger, but the attempt was a failure. The stools at the bar were all empty, the crowd consisted of two men on opposite sides of the stage, and the mirrors weren't fooling anyone.

Behind the bar, a woman was wiping glasses and racking them overhead. She was wearing an open black jacket over a lace-trimmed black bustier that gave her deep cleavage. Her chest couldn't have been on display more if she'd been holding her breasts out to me on the palms of her hands. Her blonde hair was pulled back with an elastic band and her nails were painted the color of a cosmopolitan.

I sat on a stool and asked for club soda when she came over. She thumbed one of the buttons on her dispenser and tossed in a plastic stirrer and a piece of lime while the glass filled. "Just so you know," she said, "it's a two-drink minimum to watch the show. Doesn't matter if you order club soda, I've got to charge you for wine."

"And how much is wine?"

"Ten dollars a glass."

I took a handful of bills out of my pocket, picked out a twenty and a five and put the rest back. "Must be pretty good wine."

She tapped a few spots on the screen of her cash register and then the tray shot out and my twenty disappeared inside. The five went in the pocket of her jacket.

"You can take the glass with you. Just wave when you want another."

"That's okay," I said. "I'll stay here."

"Suit yourself." She resumed her work with the glasses, drying them and tucking them away in the overhead rack.

From the far end of the room came the sound of light applause from one of the patrons. The song had ended, and in the interval before the next one began the girl onstage padded around softly, swinging her hips awkwardly in time to the silence. She was neither Mountains nor Firestone, but like the headliners she was topless and looked surgically enhanced. She also looked exhausted, but apparently there wasn't another girl to relieve her, so she kept on dancing, or anyway making enough of an effort to keep the air moving onstage.

The man seated to her left looked like a Wall Streeter on his lunch break, except that it was three in the afternoon and we were on west Twenty-fourth Street. He had an empty beer glass in front of him and a small pile of dollar bills soaking in a spill next to it. His tie was flung back over his shoulder and he kept taking his glasses off to wipe them with a paper napkin.

On the other side of the stage was the guy who had clapped at the end of the last song, and now he clapped again as the next song began. But between the beginning and end of each song, he showed his appreciation in a different way: as I watched, his hand stole into his pants through his open zipper.

I caught the bartender's attention. "Doesn't bother you that our friend there is jerking off?"

"Why? Does it bother you?"

"It's not my club."

"It's not mine either," she said.

"Yeah, but you're going to have to wash his glass."

"You want to call him on it, be my guest," she said. "Far as I'm concerned, as long as he keeps it in his pants, it's between him and whoever does his laundry."

I held my hands up. "Fair enough."

She topped off my drink, even though I had only taken a sip. "It's disgusting," she said softly, leaning forward to say it into my ear. "But, you know, this isn't exactly Scores here."

That was putting it mildly. There was top drawer and there was second rate in New York the same as anywhere else, but this wasn't even second rate, it was tenth rate. Scores was a "gentleman's club" where, between dances, you could get rare prime rib and watch hockey games on flat-screen TVs. A notch or two down, strip clubs like Flashdancers and Private Eyes dispensed with the steak but still had large dance floors and pretty girls in nice costumes, and gave the impression that they cared about the impression they gave. The Sin Factory was another animal altogether. It hurt to picture Miranda working here.

"Let me ask you something."

"I don't date customers."

"That's not it. I think you knew a friend of mine. She used to work here as a dancer."

"Yeah? Who's that?"

I drank some of my club soda. "Miranda Sugarman."

I watched as the muscles under the skin of her face tightened. "What are you, a cop or a reporter?"

"Neither," I said. "Just a friend of Miranda's."

She was trying to make up her mind whether to talk to me or throw me out of the place.

"We went to high school together," I said. "Ten years ago. She was my girlfriend."

The bartender shook her head. "I'm sorry, but I didn't know her."

"The paper said she was dancing here."

"A lot of girls dance here." She shot a glance at the dancer on the stage. "That one up there now, she's been here at least as long as your girlfriend was. But I don't know her. All I know is she calls herself 'Star,' and every day she complains about how cold it is in the dressing room."

"Is it cold?"

"Like fucking Alaska."

I stirred the ice in my glass. "What did Miranda call herself when she worked here?"

"Randy," she said. "I didn't even know her real name was Miranda. If you'd have asked me, I'd have guessed it was anything but Miranda, because why pick a stripper name that's short for your real name? I didn't know her any better than I know you."

"You never spoke to her?"

"Sure—hello, how are you, how was your Thanksgiving. Sometimes she'd be at the Derby when some of us got a bite after closing. But that was it."

"How long had she been working here?"

"I don't know, a few months? Look, I'm not going to be able to help you, I'm sorry."

"That's okay," I said. I got up to leave. "The thing is, the last time I saw her, she was heading off to college to become a doctor. I'm just trying to understand how she got from there to here."

"A doctor," the bartender said. "Jesus. All I ever gave up was being a model."

"Yeah. Well." I drank the rest of my soda. "Thanks for the wine."

The sunlight blinded me when I walked outside—I'd almost forgotten it was still day. This time of year, it wouldn't be for much longer, and once the night came, the crowds would come with it. Business would normally be light the day after New Year's, but tonight I imagined the Sin Factory would get an extra boost from rubber-neckers drawn by the story in the paper. The murder had taken place on the roof, and unless I'd missed something there was no way for patrons to get up there, but that didn't mean people wouldn't show up and try. Maybe Mandy Mountains would make a little extra on her last night in town, and if her shift hadn't ended yet, maybe that bartender would as well. But none of it would do Miranda any good.

Was that what I was trying to accomplish? I thought about this as I made my way to the subway station at Twenty-third Street. If it was, I was in for a disappointment, because nothing would do Miranda any good any more.

The 1 train carried me up to Eighty-sixth Street and from there I walked back two blocks. The red brick apartment building Miranda had lived in when we were in high school was still there, though the synagogue next to it was now a youth center with construction paper Christmas trees taped to the inside of the windows. If anyone could explain what had happened to Miranda, I figured it would be her mother—and even if she couldn't, she deserved a visit.

But when I asked in the lobby to be buzzed up, the doorman didn't know who I was talking about. Mrs. Sugarman? There was no Mrs. Sugarman in this building. 8-C? That was the Bakers. Look— And sure enough, on the intercom panel, a label said "Baker" where it had once said "Sugarman."

"You used to have a tenant named Sugarman," I said. "Is there anyone still on staff here who was working here ten years ago?"

He thought about it. "The super, maybe. You want to talk to him?"

I told him I did.

The super was a short man with a potbelly the size of a soccer ball and untrimmed grey hair around his ears. When I'd seen him last he'd had more hair, but it had already been grey. He'd just been a porter then, but seniority had apparently pushed him up the ladder. He jabbed a finger at me when he saw me and his face lit up. "Look at you! All grown up! How are you?"

I shook his hand and he dragged me into a hug. "I heard about the girl. It's terrible. Terrible. The only good thing is her mother didn't live to see it."

"What happened?"

He stepped back. "You don't know? New Year's Eve, somebody shot her."

"To her mother," I said. "What happened to Mrs. Sugarman?"

"Oh, that—that was terrible, too," he said, shaking his head. "Poor woman, six, seven years ago. Heart attack.

She was young—fifty-six, I think. But one minute to the next, just like that." He snapped his fingers. "She was trying on clothing at a store and—" He snapped his fingers again. "They found her on the floor, nothing they could do."

Six, seven years. I did the math. Miranda would just have been finishing her bachelor's degree, or maybe not even. I tried to imagine what it must have been like for her, alone, half a continent away, her only living relative suddenly gone.

"Did Miranda come back when it happened?"

"I didn't see her. All I know is when it's the end of the month, there's no rent check, and the building tells us clean it out. We threw out a lot of stuff—a sofa, table, shelves. Books, lots of books. Records. We put it all on the sidewalk, maybe someone sees something he likes, he takes it before the garbage truck comes. We paint, put in a new stove, new refrigerator. The Bakers moved in two, three weeks later."

"And you never saw Miranda again?"

"Never. Never. Except now, in the paper."

A dead end. But maybe it was also the beginning of an explanation, since whatever money Mrs. Sugarman had left Miranda, it couldn't have been a lot. And when you think about young women who start stripping, there's usually money at the root of it. Here was Miranda with maybe a year left on her undergraduate degree and a dream of going to medical school, and suddenly the single-income parent supporting her vanishes, taking the support with her. Maybe the school offered Miranda financial aid, or maybe it didn't, but either way there were living expenses to be paid, and what does an attractive twenty-year-old girl taking classes all day have to make money with other than her body at night? Oh, there were other answers, of course. She could have taken night-hour temp work filing and faxing for a law firm, or she could have flipped burgers for McDonald's. But where else could you pull down a few hundred dollars in a night, all cash? Stripping might have been the sensible, conservative alternative to turning tricks.

But this was all speculation. There had to be someone who knew what had really happened. Someone she'd known in college, someone she'd stayed in touch with from high school, someone she'd confided in when she'd returned to New York. Someone I could find if I looked hard enough.

The super reached up to put his arm across my shoulders. "So, what are you doing now? Still in school?"

"No," I said, "not for years now. I'm working."

"You work for a big company? Bank? Computers?"

I shook my head. "Small company. Investigations."

"What's that?"

"I'm a private investigator." His expression said the penny hadn't dropped yet. "A detective," I said.

"No!" He looked like he was waiting for me to laugh, tell him I was pulling his leg. I didn't. "Yes? Like in the movies?"

"Sure," I said. "Just like in the movies."

Chapter 3

On the way home, I stopped in at the office. Leo was there, going through his files. He had five piles of paper on his desk and two on the floor next to his chair. The trashcan was overflowing. My desk was neat by comparison: just one stack of case documents and half-finished paperwork and a second, smaller pile of correspondence, junk mail, and phone messages. I glanced at the messages; none was more recent than a week ago. It's not just the strip club business that slows down around the holidays.

"You go there?" Leo said without looking up from his work.

"I went."

"And?"

"It's a dive. Little hole in the wall, barely enough room for a stage. It just doesn't make sense."

"What doesn't make sense?"

"None of it makes sense, Leo. What's she doing back in New York, working as a stripper? This is a girl who . . . she didn't have to be a doctor. If that didn't work out there were plenty of things she could have done."

He didn't say anything.

"Okay, say she falls on hard times, she starts stripping. Somehow she ends up back in New York. Say that's all true. But why the hell does she end up at a place like the Sin Factory? She was too smart to work there."

"When did they start screening dancers for their IQ?"

"I just mean she would have known better. Fine, you need money, you're an attractive woman, maybe you start dancing a few nights a week—but you don't do it at a place like that, where you're lucky if someone tips you in fives instead of ones."

"Maybe she couldn't get work anywhere better."

"No, I don't buy that. She had the figure for it; she could have worked anywhere she wanted."

"Says the man who hasn't seen her in ten years." Leo put down the report he was working on and dropped his glasses on top of it. "You're going to have to face facts,

Johnny. She could have been strung out, worn down, overweight, out of her mind, she could have been a lousy dancer, you don't know."

"She was a good dancer," I said.

"Ten years ago. You don't know what she was now."

No, all I knew she was now was dead.

"I'm not asking you to help," I said.

"I'm not offering."

"I know it's a waste of time."

"Your time's my time, in case you've forgotten."

"So what's the big case you want me to work on instead? This?" I held up the phone messages. "A guy pretends to have a limp so he can collect disability from his employer?"

"It pays the bills."

"Barely. And anyway I already got the photos. What's left is just clean-up."

"What about Leventon?"

"Leventon can wait."

"She's a paying customer."

"And she can wait. A woman's dead, Leo, someone who meant a lot to me. You can't tell me to sit back and do nothing."

"What do you think you can do?"

"I don't know," I said. "But I've got to do something. What's the point of being a detective if when something like this happens you just let it?"

"Who said there was a point? It's a living, like being a dentist or fixing shoes. That's all it is."

"You don't believe that," I said. "I certainly hope you don't."

"We're private investigators. We're not cops. We don't solve murders. That's paperback novel stuff."

"At least let me look into it for a few days. I need to

put it to rest, Leo. I can't do that without knowing more."

He smeared one hand across his jaw, a gesture of defeat. "You never could," he said.

Leo Hauser was twice my age and looked older. Looking at him, you couldn't picture him as the beat cop he'd been in the seventies, walking the streets of Times Square before Disney and Giuliani made it the oversized shopping mall it was today. But he'd shown me pictures, and by God, the uniform had fit him, he'd had good posture and a steely gaze, and if that wasn't enough to make people take him seriously there'd been the couple of pounds of iron in a holster on his hip. Today—today he not only didn't look like a cop, he didn't look like the private detective he'd become. He looked like an accountant. His hair had gone white, where it hadn't just gone. You looked at him in his twelve-dollar shirts, with his glasses propped on the top of his head, and you saw an uncle at a barbecue.

But Leo was the man who had taught me this business, and along the way I'd seen what he was capable of. A lot of the time when we were hired it was by a corporation that just wanted a background check on someone they were thinking of hiring—that was the bulk of any small agency's business these days, and you did it over the phone or on the computer. But sometimes there was serious legwork to be done, and he'd done his share of it, chasing down leads and confronting the people behind them. Not recently, not so much since Arlene died—that had taken some of the chase out of him. But even now he'd insist on coming with me on a job every so often. I used to think it was his way of checking up on me, keeping an eye on the half-assed literature major he'd pulled out of NYU and tried to turn into a detective, but eventually I realized it was just his way of keeping his hand in.

When I'd shown him the article about Miranda, he'd warned me to leave it alone, and I knew he was speaking from experience. "You won't like what you find. I'll tell you that right off the bat. Whatever you find out about her, you'll wish you hadn't."

"I already wish I hadn't," I said. "I wish she was still alive, raising two kids and practicing optometry in Wisconsin. And I wish I was there with her. But what does any of that matter? I'm here, she's here, and somebody put a fucking bullet in her. I can't just sit around and wait to read about it in the paper."

"Better than ending up in the paper yourself."

"I won't."

"Better not," Leo said. "I'm too old to start again with some other kid."

I picked up a sandwich at the Korean grocery on the corner and ate it on the way home. The wind had picked up as the sun had gone down and now there was no mistaking what season we were in. People complain more about New York in the summer, the heat of August, the humidity, the clothing sticking to your back, but it's the winter that always makes me think about packing it in. Everything that's wrong with the city is still wrong in the winter, only you've got the wind chill factor to think about, too.

I climbed the four flights to my apartment and unbundled myself to the accompaniment of the hissing and clanking of my radiator. The landlord was acting out of short-lived gratitude for his Christmas tips—by February, he'd have lost interest and we'd be shivering in our kitchens again.

There was nothing on the six o'clock news, but I set my VCR to tape the eleven. You never know. Then I took a hot shower and killed some time on the Internet, tracking down every reference I could find to Miranda, the Sin Factory, or the murder. There wasn't much. Each of the local papers had covered the murder, of course, but not at great length, and details were scarce. Two gunshot wounds to the back of the head, hollow-point bullets for maximum damage. Victim pronounced dead at the scene, police were investigating. She'd been found by the club's manager, a man named Wayne Lenz, just after midnight, and he'd called an ambulance immediately on his cell phone. They'd gotten there quickly, but there's no such thing as quickly enough when you've been shot in the head with hollow point bullets.

The Sin Factory had a web site, if you could call it that: one web page showing their logo and a photo of a topless woman with one leg wrapped around a brass pole. The bullet items on the right side of the screen shouted: "Full Bar!" "Sumptuous Buffet!" and "10 Gorgeous Girls Live!!!" I couldn't imagine where they'd fit ten gorgeous girls, never mind the buffet. But then this wouldn't be the first strip club to look better on the web than it did in person.

As for Miranda herself, Google only came up with a single link, to the student directory of Rianon College in New Mexico. The link didn't work when I clicked on it. The historical copy stored in Google's archives came up just fine, but all it showed was Miranda's name on a long list of what had presumably been her classmates. She'd been in Heward Hall, room 1140, phone extension 87334. I searched the page for other instances of "1140" and found several, but only one other for Heward Hall: Jocelyn Mastaduno, extension 87333. I wrote down the name.

Then, because there was more time to kill, I did a few searches on Jocelyn Mastaduno's name. I didn't find much. One J. Mastaduno listed in Pensacola, another in Cedar Rapids. None in New York, but then why would there be? Not every pre-med at Rianon came from or ended up in New York.

Was it late enough now? I looked at the clock and decided that I wasn't in the mood to wait any longer. Lenz would either be there or he wouldn't, and either I would learn something useful or I wouldn't, but at least I'd be doing something more than just working the computer.

I had a sudden recollection, as I switched off the machine, of Miranda struggling with the PC in our computer lab—this was before the Internet, but our school had a computer elective and in our junior year we'd both taken it. I remembered sitting with her at the monitor, Miranda desperately trying to finish an assignment, me fighting with the printer when it refused to print. I finally got the thing working in time for us to be only five minutes late to class.

We wouldn't even have been five minutes late if she hadn't pushed me up against the lockers in the hallway, looked left and right to make sure we were alone, and pressed her lips to mine. "My hero," she'd said, smoothing back my hair. "Will you always be there to fix my printer for me?"

I turned off the light and returned to the Sin Factory.

Chapter 4

There was no velvet rope and the man standing at the door was wearing a leather jacket and cargo pants rather than a tux, but the music was going full blast, the lights were all lit, and it had attracted a crowd. Each time the bouncer pulled the door open, the sound of glasses being filled and emptied drifted out along with the pounding bass line of a house techno mix. While I watched from the deli next door, five people went in, one at a time, and four people came out. It was mostly businessmen, loosened ties showing under their heavy overcoats, wedding rings hidden under leather gloves, but there were also some of the low-rent types you see around any strip club, the overweight guys wearing sneakers and down coats leaking feathers at the seams. I was actually surprised to see the ratio at this place favoring the businessmen. They're the ones who can afford to go to Scores.

The bouncer stopped me at the door, one hand lightly pressing against my chest. They tell me I'll be glad later in life that I look young, and maybe it's true—Leo would probably kill to look ten years younger again. But when you're almost thirty and still get carded, the thrill escapes you.

"I was here earlier today," I said. "Nobody stopped me then." But I pulled out my wallet all the same. I could have shown him my P.I. license, I suppose, but that's rarely a good idea unless you specifically want to stir things up. I fished out my driver's license.

The bouncer turned it this way and that under the light, then handed it back. "Okay."

"Let me ask you something," I said. "Have you seen the big guy here tonight?"

"Catch?"

I didn't follow what he meant. "Lenz," I said. "Is Lenz here?"

A smile cracked open beneath the man's cheeks. I counted two gold teeth before it snapped shut again. "Yeah, Lenz is here. You don't want to be calling him 'big guy,' though."

"Why's that?"

"You ain't never met the man, have you?"

I shook my head.

"Well, you go right ahead then, call him what you want. I'll be seeing you out here again in no time." His voice was the sort of throaty growl that would be right at home coming from an idling motorcycle.

"Thanks for the tip," I said.

"What they pay me for," he said. "Preventing trouble."

The place was packed. Maybe it was all thrillseekers and newshounds, people who had come to soak up the club's sudden notoriety, but somehow that wasn't the feeling I got. The guys at the bar had the comfortable, broken-in posture of old regulars, and at the stage it was clearly Eros, not Thanatos, that was on everyone's mind.

It wasn't hard to recognize the headliners from their photos on the door. Mandy was the shorter one, and a little older than she looked in her picture, but no less well endowed. She was working the crowd, kneeling at the edge of the stage and pressing the face of one patron after another between her breasts. Her garter had a few bills in it and a few had fallen to the stage. I think one of them might have been a twenty, dropped by some high roller, but I couldn't swear to it.

Meanwhile, Rachel Firestone was back by the pole, leaning against it, doing a sort of sinuous Salome thing with her arms over her head that was completely lost on the audience. The ones who weren't slobbering on Mandy's breasts were woofing and cheering when she leaned back and bucked her hips in time to the beat.

Throughout the song she'd been playing with the bowtie knots at either hip, and now that she'd worked the crowd into a lather, she gave each knot a practiced tug and whipped off the spangled g-string entirely. This was a no-no for a club with a liquor license, but there were apparently no cops in the room, or at least none that disapproved, since she went right on bucking and twisting under the spotlight.

The song reached its climax and faded, and then it was Rachel's turn. She stepped forward as the next song started. Mandy snatched up the fallen bills, threw a few kisses to the crowd, and exited through a door at the rear of the stage. Presumably to the too-cold dressing room, where the next girl waited to take Rachel's place at the pole.

I looked around the room. The mirrored walls made it hard to get your bearings, especially since some of them turned out to be doors, like the one behind the stage. One swung open, disgorging a man wiping his hands on a twist of beige paper. Another opened to reveal a woman in heels and a clingy gown, leading a happy patron by the hand. Some sort of VIP room, presumably, which would be where the girls made their real money, extorting extra bucks for "champagne" and a private lap dance. How far things went in rooms like that depended on the club and how badly they wanted to stay on the right side of the law. Of course, I'd just gotten a hint of how law-abiding this place was. Behind closed doors, it was probably every girl for herself.

I couldn't imagine Miranda selling back room sex any more than I could imagine her dancing naked in a room like this. But then I couldn't imagine her dead of two bullets to the back of the head, either.

I felt a hand at my elbow, then a soft pressure against my arm as a woman came around from behind me. She was about my height, Chinese, in a green dress cut down the front and up the side to show a bit of this and a bit of that. The smile she gave me didn't look any more unnatural than, say, a shoe salesman's. "Hi, handsome. Want to buy me a drink?"

"I'm looking for Lenz," I said.

She dropped the smile and nodded. "He's around here, I just saw him." She looked over my shoulder, scanned the bar. "I don't know, he's probably in back. He'll be out in a minute." She patted my arm. "Back to work." And up went the smile again.

I elbowed my way to the bar, ordered my club soda, and parted with a twenty when it arrived. The woman working the tap was not the same one who'd been there earlier, but she was the same general type. If you bothered to look closely you'd see that this one had curlier hair and darker skin, that her breasts didn't fill the bustier quite so close to overflowing—but who was bothering to look? All heads in the room were turned to the stage, except for the people who were engaged in conversation with one of the women working the floor. I wasn't watching the bartender, myself—I was watching the room reflected in the mirror behind her.

But I wasn't watching closely enough, and I jumped a little when another hand landed on my elbow from behind. This one had a firm grip and didn't sweeten the pot with the soft pressure of a breast against my arm.

"I hear you're looking for me."

I turned around, then climbed down off my stool to even things out a little, but it wasn't enough. Even in boots with two-inch heels, Lenz only came up to my chin. He had unruly sideburns and something in his hair that made it shine under the room's lights. His head was tilted back and cocked at an angle and there was a stare etched onto his face that dared me to say something smart.

"Jasmine said you're looking for me. I don't think we've met. Do we have business together?"

"We might," I said. "I was Miranda Sugarman's boyfriend."

He stiffened visibly. After all he'd had to deal with, that had to be low on the list of things he wanted to hear. Still, Leo'd taught me to try the direct approach first.

"This was a long time ago, in high school," I said. "I read in the paper about what happened, and I figured maybe I could come here, talk to someone who'd known her more recently." He was doing a slow burn, which told me my chances weren't good. "I'd like to talk to you about her. Do you have a minute?"

His head twitched to the side. "Do I have a minute. No, I don't have a fucking minute. Two days, the fucking cops have been crawling up my ass, asking me questions. Your girlfriend worked here, what, four months? Gets herself killed on my premises, puts my club in the fucking paper—"

"Doesn't look like it's hurting your business any."

"The fuck do you know about my business? Jesus Christ, now I've got to talk to the fucking boyfriend from high school? What the hell are you anyway, sixteen years old? Fucking Roy'll let anyone in. Get out of here!"

Now some of the heads had turned our way. Even Rachel Firestone was watching from the stage, though she kept shimmying while she did it.

He tried to grab my arm, but I held my hands up out of his reach.

"I just want a few minutes of your time," I said.

"No, that's not what you want," Lenz said. "You want to break my balls. Well, tonight's your lucky night, since all I'm gonna do is kick you out." He marched me to the door and pushed me through, giving me a violent shove toward the curb. He turned to the bouncer, shook his index finger in the man's face. "You let him in again, you're fired. Understand?" The door slammed shut.

"Told you not to call him that," Roy said.

Chapter 5

So much for the direct approach.

I straightened myself up and took my wounded pride down the block, past the deli I'd stood in earlier, past a shuttered FedEx office, past a Radio Shack that was brightly lit but closed, to a pub that was dark but open. The sandwich board on the sidewalk outside listed dinner specials written in chalk—shepherd's pie, bangers and mash, liver and onions—along with a couple of specialty drinks and the name of the trio that played Mondays through Thursdays from nine to midnight. It was Monday, but after midnight, and both the piano and the microphone stand stood silent.

Behind the bar, a gray-haired man with rolled-up shirtsleeves and ancient blue tattoos on both forearms was wiping down the bar with a rag. He kept wiping after

I sat down and only stopped when I ordered a drink. He looked at me for a second longer than he'd have looked at most people, but in the end he didn't ask to see an ID.

"What have you got to eat this late at night?" I asked.

He set my drink down in front of me. "Anything you want, so long as it's a hamburger."

"How about a cheeseburger?"

"It'd be stretching a point," he said, "but I think the chef can manage it." He hustled off to pass the order to the kitchen.

Was this guy Keegan? I thought. Or was Keegan the owner, living somewhere down in Florida or out in Arizona while someone else managed his pub for him? Or maybe there never was a Keegan; maybe it was just a name that looked good on the sign. Didn't much matter, I supposed.

What did matter was that Keegan's Brown Derby was the only Derby in the area. I drank my drink and waited for the dancers to arrive.

The night-shift bartender showed up first, by herself. Then some of the dancers came in—I recognized Jasmine in the first group and Rachel Firestone in the second. Most of the women were wearing baggy sweats under baggier coats, their makeup washed off, their hair tucked up under knit caps. I got the sense that this is what they would have been wearing even if it had been the height of summer—anything to hide the figures they'd spent the night displaying, anything to avoid attracting the attention of the sort of stage-door johnnies who sometimes hang around at strip clubs after hours, hoping to hook up with a dancer.

Of course, I realized, that's exactly what I'd look like myself if I wasn't careful. I waited till there were eight or nine of them sitting around a pair of tables pushed together in the corner, stealing cottage fries and bits of burger from each other's plates. I came over casually, with my hands in plain view all the way.

"Sorry to bother you," I said, "but—"

"Fuck off, creep."

It was a practiced response, a reflex like kicking when the doctor taps your knee. But you could tell there was real tension behind it—you could see the stress in the eight pairs of eyes suddenly aware of me, the eight women who'd lost one of their own just forty-eight hours ago.

"Get the fuck out of here or we'll call the cops," the bartender said. "I'm not joking."

"I'm a private investigator." I took out my wallet and this time I did fish out my P.I. license. Maybe they couldn't read it from where they were sitting, but they could see that I was holding up a laminated card with the state seal on it. That was something, I suppose.

"I'm investigating the death of Miranda Sugarman. I would appreciate your help."

"You were in the club tonight." This was from Rachel, who was at the table closer to me. She held my eye as she said it.

"That's right."

"You're the guy Lenz threw out."

"Yes."

"You said you were her boyfriend," the bartender said. "Was that just a line?"

"No, that was the truth. I knew her ten years ago. We went to high school together."

There was silence around the tables. They'd stopped picking at their food.

"Did any of you know her?" I asked.

Jasmine spoke up. "We worked the C shift together last week. First time I met her."

"Did she say anything to you that seemed strange? Anything that might explain what happened?" Jasmine shook her head. "Anyone else?"

"She didn't talk much," one of them said, and a few of the others nodded. "Just came in, did her sets, got dressed, and left."

"Someone told me she ate with you here sometimes."

"Once, maybe. I don't remember her saying two words to anyone."

"Did she have any regular customers? Were there people who came just to see her?"

No one seemed to remember any.

I looked from face to face and saw the same things in each of them. Fear, distrust, but also a sort of cautious wishfulness, as though they hoped I was for real and not just some scam artist. Rachel especially—she watched me more intently than the others and seemed to be mulling something over. But whatever it was, she didn't come out with it.

I took out a handful of business cards with my name and phone number on them, handed them to Rachel who dealt them out around the table. "My name is John Blake," I said, "and you've got my cell phone number there. You remember anything, anything at all, please call me. If something happens—anything at all—call me. Okay?" A few of them nodded.

"Mr. Blake," one of them said as I turned to leave, and I turned back. "Do you think it's going to happen again? I mean, do you think it's someone going after dancers? Or was it just her?"

I thought about the two bullets to the back of the head. A classic execution, Leo had called it. Maybe a little bloodier than average—a pair of hollow-points fired at point-blank range would tear half your face off—but still, it wasn't the sort of thing you'd expect from a serial killer or someone getting a sexual thrill from the act.

God knows these women wanted and deserved some reassurance, and standing there I wanted to give them some. But what if I did, and they let down their guard, and then it turned out I was wrong?

"I don't know," I said. "I'm sorry."

I walked back past the club, which was dark and locked up tight behind a metal gate. The Sin Factory filled the ground floor of a three-story brownstone, and I assumed the whole building was theirs—I couldn't imagine unrelated tenants living above a club like this, if only because of the noise. Although in New York, you never knew.

There was a narrow passage at the side of the building, wide enough for a stack of overstuffed Hefty bags filled with the night's refuse. The garbage trucks would be here in a few hours, and in the meantime the rats could enjoy their own buffet.

I edged past the garbage and came out in a little rear courtyard, lit by the feeble glow of a sixty-watt bulb over the door. There was graffiti all over the rear wall and dark stains along the base. The door had a plate for a Medeco deadbolt in addition to the standard Rabson cylinder above the knob, and though I was tempted to try to pick them and get inside, I'd learned enough over the past six years not to bother. In the movies you always see people opening locks like it's nothing, but the truth is it's easier to take a door off its hinges than it is to pick a Medeco.

Besides, there were other ways in, if in was where I wanted to be. There was a fire escape running up the rear wall. There were only slightly taller buildings on either side, and the odds were they didn't both have Medeco locks. And if they did, there were more short buildings on either side of them—it was probably how the killer had gotten onto the roof and then gotten away afterwards.

But what would I see if I went there now? I could go to the roof and see where Miranda had died, maybe get a feeling for what it had been like there that night, but if I was thinking of searching for clues, I could forget it. The NYPD would have picked it clean. They'd certainly have done a better job than I could do at two in the morning with no light.

I went out the way I'd come in, my back to the wall, trying not to inhale the sour smell of the trash. On the street, traffic was light and none of the cars that passed me were empty cabs, so I walked to the train station and rode the 1 downtown. When I came up out of the subway, my phone beeped in its plastic holder on my hip. The screen showed a little picture of an envelope with a letter "V" next to it. I found an empty doorway, thumbed in •86 and my password.

"Mr. Blake? This is Rachel Firestone. We met earlier tonight? I was hoping to talk to you. I guess you're not there." I waited, but that seemed to be the end of the voicemail. Either Verizon had cut her off or she'd run out of things to say. But then I heard her voice again. "Listen, there's no good number where you can reach me. Why don't you come to the Derby tomorrow at six—I don't go on until eight, and we can talk. Okay? Okay. See you then."

I played the message again when I got upstairs and then once more after getting undressed, but it didn't say any more to me either time. There was nothing I could do about it but wait.

I didn't want to—I wanted to get up, get on the computer, and chase down a dozen leads. I wanted to bang on some doors until someone told me why Miranda Sugarman was lying in the morgue. But it was almost three in the morning now, I was exhausted, and Miranda wasn't going anywhere. I forced myself to lie down, close my eyes, and try to get some sleep.

Chapter 6

In the morning, I made some toast and a cup of coffee and started working the phone. The only thing that slowed me down was having to wait till noon to reach offices on the West Coast.

Neither of the Mastadunos I'd found was Jocelyn—one was Jessica, the other Jerome—and neither of them knew a Jocelyn. I left a message with the Rianon alumni office, asking for their help. I logged on to the Internet again and copied down the names of the girls who'd been in all the other rooms on the eleventh floor of Heward Hall, and while I was at it the ones on the tenth and the twelfth. Some were named Smith and Jones or the equivalent, but others had more obscure names and I started hunting them down through public directories. I found a Lainie Burroughs in Midland, Wisconsin, and it was the right Lainie Burroughs, but she hadn't known either Miranda or Jocelyn. I found Maya Eskin. I found Jody Sinkiewicz. Jody remembered Jocelyn and both of them remembered Miranda, but neither had any idea what had become of them.

"They were really close," Jody said, "I remember

that, I'd always see them in the hall together. I mean, I didn't see them all that often, but if I saw one of them, I saw them both. And then for a long time I didn't see either of them and I asked someone, and she said they'd dropped out."

"Who told you that?"

"God, who was it. Was it Katherine? Probably Katherine, she knew them better than I did."

"What's Katherine's last name?"

"It's Lewis now, but then it was Chin."

"Do you know where I can reach her?"

"Yeah, hold on." From the other end of the phone came the sound of a clasp being opened, pages being turned. "Katherine Lewis, she's in Chicago now, working at the Children's Hospital? I can give you her work number."

"Thank you."

I got numbers, I got names. I checked names off my list and I added new names to it. Call by call, a picture started to grow, a picture of Miranda that was half familiar and half alien. She hadn't had many friendships, but the few she'd had had been exceptionally tight. She'd been an A student in high school but did poorly in her freshman year at Rianon, and her grades didn't get better after that. She hadn't dated anyone. Or maybe she had— there were conflicting stories. She started rooming with Jocelyn in the second semester of her sophomore year, and a year later they both left the school. There was a rumor that they'd dropped out to go on the road, drive across the country or maybe up to Canada, but nobody knew for sure.

Eventually, a man from the alumni office called me back. They'd already talked to the police and weren't comfortable sharing information with anyone else. Could they at least confirm that Miranda and Jocelyn had dropped out before the start of their senior year? No, he was afraid that was personal information. Did they have an address for Jocelyn? That would be personal information, too. Could they at least pass a message to her if they did have an address? Grudgingly, he agreed, so I wrote a brief note and faxed it to him. I didn't have high hopes.

But that's the nature of the detective business. Nothing you do has especially good odds of working, but if you do enough things, make enough calls and knock on enough doors, eventually something will work. Or that's the idea, anyway.

By two, my shoulder hurt from gripping the phone and I'd run out of people to call, so I switched to the computer. Search engines like Google are only a starting point, though they're a good one; when you're in the business, you become familiar with all the other resources out there, ones that allow you to track down municipal filings, business filings, deeds, insurance data, court records, and the like. I tracked through all of them, keeping one eye on the clock. Four hours seems like a long time, but the Internet eats hours like a kid eats popcorn.

Miranda hadn't left much of a trail—she hadn't been sued, hadn't been arrested, hadn't been fingerprinted. She hadn't started a business, hadn't taken out loans, or at least none that I could find a record of. Jocelyn was similarly blank. They were just two kids who stepped out of their dorm room one morning and into the ether.

But Wayne Lenz and the Sin Factory were another story. No shortage of paper on the club, of course: you can't run a nightclub, strippers or no strippers, without filing plenty of forms. But searching on Lenz turned up a nice pile of material, too.

I looked at his pinched features staring out at me from the screen. Born in Ohio in 1959, where he was remanded to the custody of an aunt after his parents made local headlines by driving off a bridge. Apparently moved to New York as a teenager, since he started having run-ins with the NYPD as early as 1978. Two charges in one year: aggravated assault, though he was only given probation, and then, late in the year, mail fraud. The details of the fraud charge were opaque, as criminal court records so often are, but it looked like he'd tried his hand at running a con and had done a lousy job of it. He'd gotten a five-year sentence and served two. Kept his head down in the eighties, only to surface again in a drug bust in '93. Back in prison, out in four.

And then he'd bought the Sin Factory? No, the club's SICA filings made it clear that Lenz was just an employee. The business was owned by a limited liability company set up in Delaware, GoodLife LLC, whose only listed address was a P.O. box. And the man behind GoodLife? He didn't seem to like to sign his name to things, but in this day and age it takes a lot of work to stay anonymous. All it takes is one slip to blow it, and Leo and I had seen people a lot slicker than this guy. After hunting for about an hour I found a loose thread to pull on: the administrative contact listed in the registration records for the domain name of the Sin Factory's one-page web site. A man named Mitchell Khachadurian with a New Jersey phone number.

I waited while the phone rang seven, eight times, then heard an out-of-breath voice pick up on the ninth ring. "Yeah? Hello?"

"Mr. Khachadurian?"

"Yes? Who is this?"

"This is officer Michael Stern of Midtown South in Manhattan," I said. "We're following up on a disturbance at the Sin Factory—"

"You people have got to stop calling me. I'm not involved with my brother's business, I don't know anything about it, and I don't want to know."

"Your name is listed as a contact for your brother's web site."

"I begged him to take that off," he said. "I made that site three years ago. Listen, I haven't even talked to Murco in a year."

"Mr. Khachadurian, do you know how we could reach Murco?"

He snorted. "You guys probably know better than I do. You certainly see him more."

"What's the last number you had for him?"

He had to think for a second, but then he rattled off a 917 number. A cell phone, presumably. I wrote it down.

"If you talk to him," Mitchell said, "don't mention you got his number from me, okay?"

"You've got my word of honor," I said, "as a policeman."

I made it through the door at six on the dot, but Rachel wasn't there yet. The same old man was behind the bar, and he recognized me from the previous night. "Another cheeseburger? Chef's got some practice with it now."

"No, thanks. Just a coke."

He filled a glass and set it down on a napkin, dropped in a straw. "Saw you were talking to the girls last night. They're a good bunch," he said. "Don't have an easy lot in life."

"No," I said.

"They come in here for some peace and quiet, and I'm

glad to give it to them. They need a place to let off steam, feel safe. I wouldn't keep the place open so late nights, only where would they go if I didn't?"

I nodded.

"Time to time," he said, "people see them here, figure out who they are, and start dropping by. Think maybe they can make friends, or pick up some company for the night, have a little fun. They don't encourage it, and neither do I."

He shot some more coke into my glass now that the foam had settled.

"You seem like a nice fellow, clean cut, well dressed, that's why I'm talking to you like this. There's some you talk to and some it's not worth the breath, you've got to find other ways to get through to those."

"I hear you," I said. "The girls won't have any trouble from me."

"Ah, that's good," he said. "We've got to look out for one another in this world, don't we?"

So where were you, I wanted to ask, when Miranda needed someone to look out for her? But all I said was, "That we do."

I saw Rachel come through the door then, look around the room, and spot me at the bar. She was wearing jeans and a cardigan, with a hat pulled down over her ears. She took the hat off and shook out her hair as she walked over.

"Don't break my kneecaps," I said. "She asked me to meet her here."

We sat in the back, at the table farthest from the door. Even so, Rachel kept darting glances over her shoulder.

"Thanks for meeting me. I wasn't even sure you got my message."

"I'm sorry I missed your call. I was on the subway."

"That's okay."

We were both silent for a bit. She had something to say, and I figured she'd say it when she was ready. In the meantime, I didn't want to open my mouth and maybe scare her off by saying the wrong thing.

"The reason I asked you to meet me is, Randy talked to me the night before she was shot," she finally said. "She was terrified. She told me she was afraid someone was going to kill her."

"Did she say who?"

"Yes," Rachel said. "Murco Khachadurian."

Chapter 7

Her hands were shaking. I fought the urge to reach across the table and cover them with my own.

"It's not like we knew each other," she said. "We didn't. I'd just come from three weeks at a club in Jersey called Carson's. Right on the other side of the bridge?"

I nodded.

"So who am I to her? Just the new girl, right?" She swallowed some of her drink, stirred the rest with the little red straw. "We'd never talked before. Not one word. But we were changing after the last set, it was just the two of us in the dressing room, and I guess she just needed to talk to someone. God. I wish I'd said something to someone, but I didn't think she was serious. No, that's not it—she was serious. I just didn't believe it was true."

"What did she say?"

Rachel closed her eyes tight. I've noticed that some people do that when they're trying hard to remember, though for others it seems to be a matter of not wanting to look you in the eyes while they tell a whopper. "She said, 'There are bad things going on at this club,' and I said something like, 'You're saying it's a high-mileage place?' and she said no, that it was much worse."

"High mileage?"

"You know, lots of touching." She looked at me, and I got the feeling that she was suddenly noticing how young I looked—nice and clean-cut, as my friend at the bar had said—and maybe wondering how much I knew about the ways of the world. "Some clubs, there's a strict hands-off policy, look but don't touch—that's no mileage. Some places, the dancers are expected to grind a little during a lap dance, but the guys have to keep their pants on and their hands to themselves. That's low mileage. Then there are places where the whole point is to make the guy come. Basically they can touch you anywhere except inside your g-string, and you can do anything to get them off short of actually having sex with them."

"And that's high mileage."

She nodded. "Only thing higher's full service. Most girls won't work for a high-mileage club, but sometimes you don't know going in, because the high-mileage stuff is going on in the champagne rooms, not out front. So girls will warn each other, especially when you're new to a club, and I figured that's what Randy was doing."

"But it wasn't."

"No. She said, 'Believe me, you'll be glad when someone comes in and all he wants is a hand job.' And I said, 'What? What is it? Is it S&M?' Because some of these places, that's the big secret, they've got a dungeon in the basement and guys come in to get whipped. I've never understood that stuff myself, but it doesn't bother me—I'd rather smack someone with a riding crop than jerk him off. But she said, 'No, it isn't sex. It's drugs.' "

"Drugs?"

"That's what she said. She had this whole story about how the guy who owns the club is a dealer and is using the girls to move his merchandise, and if you don't go along with it or you talk to anyone about it, you wind up in a ditch in Jersey City."

"But here she was talking to you about it."

"Right, exactly," Rachel said, "and I was thinking, this girl's watched one too many re-runs of *The Sopranos*. Because that's the vibe she was giving off. Real drama queen. The people you meet in this business are not exactly the most stable—" A look of embarrassment washed over her face. "I'm sorry."

"It's okay."

"But you used to date her."

"It was a long time ago," I said.

We didn't say anything for a bit. Rachel brushed her hair out of her eyes, and for a moment I was reminded of Miranda. They didn't look anything alike, but something about the gesture brought her to mind—that and the fact that I'd seen this woman dancing naked on a stage the night before, and here she was now, looking completely normal, completely ordinary. It was like a photographic negative of my experience with Miranda.

I also found myself noticing how, without the stage makeup and the gel in her hair and all the other trappings of her trade, Rachel was a very beautiful woman. Maybe this shouldn't have come as a surprise, but it did. Dancing on stage she'd been just another pin-up, another pair of high heels and long legs and bare breasts, and I'd found nothing very erotic about the sight. But

across a table in a pub at twilight, dressed in faded jeans and a sweater the color of ginger ale, she was an ordinary woman, and infinitely more appealing.

"What did Miranda say she was afraid of?"

"She told me she'd found out about the drugs and somehow had gotten on the wrong side of the owner, this Khachadurian, and now she was sure he was going to kill her. She really sounded scared. But you know, lots of girls talk themselves into getting scared or angry or ashamed over all sorts of things, and maybe one tenth of it is real. So I just tried to make her feel better. I remember saying, 'I'm sure it's not that bad. You haven't told anyone, right? So what reason would he have to do anything to you?' And then a day later, she's dead."

"It may not be related," I said. But even as I said it, I knew how foolish it sounded.

"The terrible thing," Rachel said, "is when I heard what had happened, the first thing I thought about wasn't her, it was, 'She told me, and now they're going to come after me, too.' "

"And?"

She shook her head. "Nothing's happened. So far, anyway. I've got six nights left and then I can move on, and you'd better believe I'm not coming back. I thought about quitting early, but I don't want to do anything to rock the boat."

"Do you know if it's true, what Miranda said about the owner? Are the dancers moving drugs for him?" An image from the prior night came back to me, the businessmen in suits, coming and going, when you'd normally expect a more downscale crowd at a club like the Sin Factory. The addition of drugs to the picture went a long way toward explaining what guys with money in their wallets might be doing there.

"I haven't seen it. Of course, maybe they stopped after the murder because there were police all over the place. I wasn't there long enough before it happened, I wouldn't necessarily have seen it."

"Have you seen anything else?"

"Like what?"

"Anything that made you uneasy."

She laughed, but the laugh itself was an uneasy one. "Nothing worse than at Carson's."

"That bad?"

"They're all the same. Unless you look like Jennifer Lopez or a Playboy centerfold—maybe then the places you get to work at are different. Although actually I doubt it. I'm sure the money's better, but the management and the customers, I don't know."

"Better quality leather in the whips," I said.

"Exactly."

"Have you ever met Khachadurian?"

"I only saw him once, on my first day," she said. "Lenz was walking with this huge guy, took up half the hallway. One of the other girls said that's who it was."

"And Lenz? What's he like in private?"

"The same. In private, in public, he's a prick. He's the same with everyone as he was with you last night." I heard a muted beeping from under the table, the sound of a cell phone picking out the notes to Ravel's *Bolero*. She picked up her handbag, dropped it on the table, and rooted around in it until she found her phone.

"Go ahead, take it," I said. "I'll step over there."

"No, it's not a call. I just set the alarm." She pressed a button on the side of the phone and the melody stopped. "I need to go. I'm sorry. I've got to get changed and get ready." Her hands were shaking again. Or maybe they'd never stopped.

"How can I contact you if I need to?" I said

She still had her cell phone in her hand, so I would have thought the answer was obvious; but then again, I also remembered her saying in her voicemail that there was no good number where I could reach her.

"I'm sorry," she said again. "I just don't give my personal number out to anyone. I mean, like, four people have it. You seem like a normal guy, but I don't know you."

"You're absolutely right," I said, and I meant it. The more careful she was, the better. "You've got my number. Call me if anything happens. If I need to get in touch with you, how about I leave a message for you here?"

She nodded, and got up. "John—" She lowered her voice. "Do you think Randy was right? Part of me thinks she was just making this stuff up and now I'm getting sucked into her fantasy. But someone killed her, and if it's the guy I'm working for, I could be in real danger."

This time the reassurance came out before I could stifle it. "I think you're pretty safe, Rachel. Even if he did kill her—and I don't know, it doesn't sound right, why would he do it on the roof of his own building?—but even if he did, I don't think he's going to try it again anytime soon, not while the police are watching the place. You're probably safer there than anywhere in the city."

She nodded, wanting to believe. Then she said, quietly, "It's Susan."

"What?"

"You called me Rachel. That's for the clubs. My name's Susan." She held her hand out, and this time I took it.

I watched her go, then paid the check and left myself. The streets were dark, or anyway as dark as it ever gets in Manhattan. Storefronts kept the avenue well lit, but on the side streets it was another story. Streetlamps left pools of light at regular intervals up and down the sidewalk, but outside these pools it was all shadows.

I stepped out between two parked cars and walked in the street itself. I don't know why I do this. It's not clear that it reduces my risk—if anything, it adds the risk of getting run down by a car to whatever risk of a bad encounter I might have on the sidewalk. But somehow it makes me feel safer when I'm not hemmed in by shuttered buildings on one side and empty cars on the other.

Tonight I had it easy: there were no people and no cars. You could hear some honking in the distance, and occasionally the squeal of a set of tires gripping the pavement, but that was in the distance. This block was mine and mine alone.

Halfway between Eighth and Seventh Avenues, my cell phone rang. At first I couldn't make out the voice of the man on the other end, but when I covered my other ear his voice became clearer.

"—my daughter. Mr. Blake? Are you there?"

"I'm here. Who is this?"

"Daniel Mastaduno. You sent a fax with your phone number on it. Is this a bad time to call?"

"No, it's fine," I said. It took a second for the name to click. Mastaduno. The roommate. "Your daughter is Jocelyn Mastaduno?"

"That's right."

"Where is she? Can I talk to her?"

"I was hoping you could tell me. We haven't heard from Jocelyn in six years, Mr. Blake. Do you have any idea where she is?"

Six years? "No," I said. "I—"

The punch came from behind, and it landed square in my kidney. The phone flew from my hand and clattered against the door of a car. I dropped to my knees and took a boot in the stomach that knocked out of me what little breath I'd had left. Another kick dug deep into my gut, and then another. My chest was pounding and my side was screaming with pain. I wanted to move, but I couldn't. I couldn't breathe. It was all I could do to keep from throwing up.

Ten feet away, my phone lay on its side, chirping, "Hello? Hello? Mr. Blake?"

A gloved hand gripped my hair, pulled my head off the ground. I felt a pair of lips brush my ear. "Leave it alone, man, or next time they'll make me give you more than a warning."

The hand laid my head down gently. The cell phone was silent now. No cars came.

Chapter 8

The look of pity Leo gave me was almost worse than the beating.

"How do you let a guy get close enough to you to land a punch without noticing?"

"I was on the phone, I told you."

"Goddamn cell phones," he said, "how many times have I told you—"

"Lots of times. It's enough."

"It's not enough! Look at you!"

"Leo, please. I want you to put me in touch with someone who can tell me about Murco Khachadurian. Someone on the force."

"Anyone I knew on the force retired five years ago, and I'll tell you something else—if I did know someone, I wouldn't ask him to help you. I'm not going to help you go and get yourself killed."

"I'm not going to get myself killed."

"Stand up and say that," he said.

I was lying flat on my back on the leather couch in our reception area. I'd made it to the office because it was closer to the Sin Factory than my apartment, and getting in didn't require me to climb any stairs. Spending the night on the couch had left me with a stiff neck that I hadn't had before, but at least the pain in my stomach was a little less intense. My side still felt like someone was sticking in a knife in me any time I turned, and standing up was out of the question.

Leo had found an old hot water bottle in the bottom of one of his desk drawers and he'd filled the thing with water he'd heated in the coffee maker. It had gone cold in the meantime, but it was too much trouble to get it out from under me. He'd also fed me a glass of whiskey, and between the red rubber pad under my back and the rocks tumbler in my hand, I felt like my own grandfather.

"Khachadurian's involved," I said. "Whether he killed Miranda or not, he's part of what happened, and I'm going to talk to him."

"What are you going to do, call him on your cell phone?"

"Yes. That's exactly what I'm going to do. I got a number for him from his brother, and if that doesn't work I'll get another number somewhere else."

"I should never have trained you," Leo said.

"Leo, I'm going to find the man and I'm going to talk to him, and if he killed Miranda, I'm going to bring him in. All I'm asking is, before I make the call, I want to know more about him. The more I know, the better the chances I come out of it in one piece."

"Have another drink."

I set my glass down on the floor. "I don't want another drink. I didn't even want the first one. All I want is some information. If you don't help me, I'll get it some other way. But don't tell me you can't get it because you don't know anyone anymore. You're not that out of touch."

Leo took the glass, refilled it, and put it back within arm's reach. "Here's a deal. When you can make it to the bathroom on your own, no promises, but I'll make a few calls."

I tried to sit up, winced as the pain shot through me.

"When," Leo said.

"Yeah. When." I lay back down.

By midday, I could stand on my own, as long as I leaned against the back of a chair. At one, Leo brought me a turkey sandwich and a Snapple, and at three I was leaning against the bathroom door, pissing it away. It was excruciating. But I came back from the bathroom as proud of myself as a newly toilet-trained toddler.

"Zip up," Leo said.

"You'll want to start making those calls now," I said.

I went back to the couch while he went into the other room to work the phone. The truth was that he probably didn't know anyone still on the force—his contemporaries were all out of the game one way or the other, retired or dead, and even the rookies who'd shaken his hand at his retirement party were probably coming up on their own. But his buddies had had kids, and the police force is one of the last great dynastic employers: if your daddy was a cop, there was a good chance you'd go into the Academy yourself when the time came. So, no, Bill

O'Malley, Leo's partner for his first five years, wasn't around any more, but Bill, Jr. was. Leo would be able to get someone on the phone.

That left me to hold up my end of the bargain, and with Leo in the other room, I didn't have to put a brave face on it any more. The truth was I felt like shit. I could walk again, and I didn't think anything inside me was torn or broken, but my God, it couldn't have hurt any more if something had been. I thought about the man who'd done it. Until he'd spoken, I couldn't be sure who it was, but the voice wasn't one you'd forget. I'd been bounced by the Sin Factory's bouncer, and that meant either Lenz or maybe Khachadurian himself had told him to do it. Which meant I was in their sights already.

It didn't mean for sure that Rachel—Susan—was right. It didn't mean that Khachadurian had put the bullets in the back of Miranda's head or given the order to do so. All it meant for sure was that they didn't want me poking around and maybe bringing to light whatever dirty business they were carrying on behind the closed doors of the champagne rooms. Maybe it was just sex, not drugs, or maybe it was both, but that didn't necessarily mean it was murder, too.

Not necessarily.

But as Susan had said, *someone* had killed Miranda, and the little I'd heard about Khachadurian so far didn't make him sound like an unlikely candidate.

I fiddled with my cell phone while I waited for Leo to come back. Overnight, the battery had drained and I didn't have a charger in the office. But I'd get it working again. The faceplate was scuffed and scratched, but it didn't look like the damage was serious. They built those things to take a beating. Wish I could say the same for myself.

I thought about what Dave Mastaduno had been saying to me when we'd been interrupted. No, not Dave. Daniel. What Daniel Mastaduno had been saying: *We haven't heard from Jocelyn in six years, Mr. Blake.* Rianon must have forwarded my fax after all. I tried to imagine what it had been like for him to get it. Six years of silence, and then out of the blue one day a fax comes from a stranger with your daughter's name on it. A little like waking up one morning and seeing Miranda in the newspaper. A name from the past, a face from the past, all your worst fears brought to life.

Was Jocelyn Mastaduno dead, too? Or was she just missing? Or hiding? Or maybe she just didn't want to talk to her parents—God knows I hadn't talked to my father in more than six years, though once a year we exchanged chilly Christmas cards. There wasn't necessarily a big mystery here. And yet somehow I had a bad feeling about it, as though Miranda's death was poisoning everything else around her.

Leo opened the door, shut it quietly behind him, and held up a slip of paper. He made me walk all the way across the room to take it from him, and I forced myself to do it without grimacing and without holding onto the chairs along the way.

"What I wouldn't give to be your age again. Take a beating at night, ready to run a marathon the next morning."

I snatched the paper, saw the phone number for the Midtown South Precinct house. I didn't recognize the extension. "O'Malley?"

"No, Stan Kirsch's son. Kirby, and you tell me, what's a worse name than that for a guy named Kirsch?"

"Leo."

"Leo Kirsch? What's wrong with that?"

"Leo."

"What?"

"Thank you."

He sat down at his desk, didn't look at me. "Can't let you fuck up on your own," he said. "I've got too much invested in you."

I took a deep breath before climbing the stairs and had to stop for another at each landing, but eventually I made it to my apartment. My cell phone would take hours to charge completely, so I got it going and used the phone by my bed to call Kirby Kirsch.

"John. Yeah. I got the message you'd be calling. I think your dad knew my dad?"

"Leo's not my dad. He's my boss. But yes, he used to work with your dad, I think in the late seventies."

"That's when it would have had to be," he said, "since my dad never made it into the early eighties."

"What happened?"

I heard him chew something and swallow. "Shooter at a street fair, took out two pedestrians and two policemen before blowing his own brains out."

"Jesus," I said. "I'm sorry."

"Yeah. Me, too. But that's the job." Some more chewing came over the line. This one had a thick hide, all right.

"Did the message say what I'm calling about?"

"Just that you'd call."

"Someone I used to know was shot a few nights ago, a woman named Miranda Sugarman."

"Sugarman, that's the stripper?"

"That's what she was now. Ten years ago, she was my girlfriend when we were in high school." This was his turn to say *Sorry*, but he didn't. "We're looking into it—"

"We?"

"I work for Leo's agency. We're just trying to find out some more."

"For the family?"

"There's no family," I said. "It's for me."

"What do you want to know?"

"Someone told me the club she was working at is owned by a man named Murco Khachadurian, and he sounds like a bit of a questionable character."

"He's a fucking scumbag, is what he is."

"Yeah. Well. That's what I was hoping you could tell me about."

"There are two of them, Little Murco and Big Murco, the son and the father, and they're both scumbags."

"Connected?"

"They wish. The son's just a thug, and the father, he's a 'businessman,' which means he made some money in some legitimate racket, Armenian carpets or something, and now he's always trying to cut himself in on deals that are bigger than he is, make a big score."

"Drugs?"

"Drugs, some schlock, some grey market booze, whatever he can get a piece of."

"You ever bust him?"

"He's small potatoes. We keep an eye on him to see if he'll lead us to someone bigger."

"And the murder?"

"Sugarman? There were forty people in the club at midnight, girls and customers and the bartender and the janitor, and any of them could have done it."

"Not Khachadurian?"

"He's probably never set foot in the club."

"I don't mean personally."

"Well, when we find the person who pulled the

trigger, we'll ask whether someone put him up to it."

"What do you think?"

"What do I think? You talk about strippers, hookers, massage parlor girls, it's almost always another girl who does it. They hate each other. 'She used my lipstick. She took my customer. I saw her going through my locker.' Either that or a john, some guy she rubbed the wrong way, or maybe the right way but he's fucked up with guilt feelings about the whole thing. One or the other, that's your killer nine times out of ten."

"And the tenth time?"

He was silent for a moment. "How long have you been working for Leo?" he said

"Why?"

"Ask him. In this job, you don't worry about the tenth time. When it comes it comes, but most cases it doesn't and you don't worry about it before you have to."

Leo had told me. He'd told me plenty of times. All the cop wisdom this guy had, Leo had double, and he'd been pouring it in my ear since the day he plucked me out of NYU to be his part-time research assistant. I knew all about the nine times out of ten and the standard procedures and the steps the police would be taking to solve the crime. I also knew a murdered stripper wouldn't be at the top of their priority list and that any one-off violent crime that wasn't solved in the first forty-eight hours was likely to stay unsolved forever. Every day brought a dozen more, and there were only so many cops to go around.

I also knew that Kirby Kirsch was right, that if anything was going to work, it was probably going to be the standard procedure, and that there was no point in inventing complicated explanations for a crime that was probably very simple. I knew all this, but it didn't do any good.

"You think I could see the body?" I said.

"You don't want to," he said. "Not if you used to go out with her. We're talking chopped meat, man. There wasn't even enough left for a good dental—we had to go to her apartment for a DNA match."

The guy was still eating. I listened to him chew.

"Thanks for talking to me," I said. I tried hard to keep my voice level. "I appreciate your taking the call."

"Leo still carries some weight around here. A lot of people remember him."

"I'll tell him," I said. "It'll make his day."

I carefully stripped off my clothes and got under the hottest shower I could stand.

When I moved in, I'd bought one of those three-speed massaging showerheads but I'd never used more than the one speed it came set on, the one that came at you like water out of a watering can. Now I turned it to the one that felt like a thousand tiny needles and let it go to work on my back. There was a fist-sized bruise on my right side, plum-colored and tender to the touch, but it was starting to go yellow at the edges and wasn't the source of shooting pain it had been before. I'd live.

I thought about the other bruises I'd gotten over the past half decade of working for Leo, that and the threats, the fights I'd only narrowly talked my way out of, the dirt I'd dug up on people who'd wanted to keep it hidden. How had I ended up doing this for a living? Around the time Miranda had been making plans to become a doctor, what was it I thought I'd be doing? I couldn't remember. But it wasn't this. I did remember the day I met Leo, and the day I joined him full-time because it was either that or go to work for an Internet company and I still had some self-respect. I'd never wanted to do this for a living, but I couldn't remember wanting to do anything else either, and after a while, it was the only thing I'd ever done.

It was a living, as Leo had said—but not like being a dentist or fixing shoes. It was more like being a stripper, I imagined. Even if you took pride in doing your job well, you ended up feeling dirty at the end of the day.

So why did I do it? I didn't know how to do anything else, but there was another side to it as well. I did it because somebody had to. Someone had to stand up for people like Miranda. It was the sort of thought you could only entertain in the shower, or in bed when you were on the verge of falling asleep, and even then not for long. Look too closely at it and it would embarrass you. But on days when I had nothing else, it gave me a reason to keep going into the office in spite of the bruises and the people I had to deal with and the general feeling that I was pitching my tent in a sewer.

When I turned off the water, I heard my cell phone going, the vibration rattling the base of the charger against the top of my desk. I didn't bother toweling off and walked as quickly as I could, snatching up the phone before whoever was calling could hang up.

"Mr. Blake?"

I recognized the voice. "Mr. Mastaduno. Hold on a second." I slipped into a pair of pants and a sweatshirt I'd left draped over the chair. The last thing I needed was to catch a cold on top of everything else. "I'm back. I'm sorry about last night—"

"What happened?"

"Just some business I had to take care of. Let's talk about your daughter."

"What do you know about her?"

"I don't—just that she was once the roommate of a

woman named Miranda Sugarman, who was killed in New York on New Year's Eve. I wanted to talk to Jocelyn to see if she could tell me anything about Miranda."

"Oh." I could hear the man deflating over the phone. "I was hoping . . . It's been so long."

"Can you tell me what happened?"

"I don't know. I honestly just don't know. She was at school. She was doing fine, or anyway that's what we assumed. And then . . . "

"And then?"

"We got a call from the dean's office saying she had turned in a leave-of-absence form and when we tried calling her, the phone was disconnected. We tried her roommate, but that phone was shut off, too. We called some of the other girls whose names Jocelyn had mentioned, but no one knew where she'd gone, just that she'd gone off with her roommate, this Sugarman. That was six years ago, Mr. Blake. Not one phone call since then, not a letter, not a postcard. Nothing. We figured she'd come back, here if not to school, but no. Her mother's been sick with worry, I've been sick with worry—not one word."

"Had you been close before that?"

"Close? Your own daughter, that's as close you can get."

"Did you ever hire anyone to try to find her?"

"Yes, after about three months. We hired Serner, because someone told us they were the best."

"They are."

"I might as well have thrown my money out the window. They would send these reports, pages and pages of 'We went here,' 'We went there,' 'We talked to him,' 'We talked to her'—but they didn't find my daughter. That's what we were paying them to do."

"I understand."

"Do you? Do you? It's been six years, Mr. Blake. I don't sleep. My wife is grey. Completely grey. My daughter's gone. When you sent your fax . . ."

"I'm sorry," I said. "I didn't mean to make things worse."

"You didn't make them worse, it's just . . . We'd stopped hoping, you know?"

I wanted to say, At least your daughter's not dead. But maybe she was, and if she wasn't, was that necessarily better? For her certainly, but for her parents?

On the other hand, maybe knowing would be better than not knowing.

"I don't want to get your hopes up," I said, "since I probably won't find anything. If Serner couldn't, I probably can't either. But I'll try, and if you give me your number, I'll call you with anything I find out." Mastaduno gave me a Westchester number and I scrawled it down under Kirby Kirsch's. "One other thing, could you tell me who you worked with at Serner? Maybe I can get something out of them."

"The man we dealt with was William Battles. Do you want his phone number? I can look it up."

Bill Battles. No, that was one phone number I didn't need.

"That's okay," I said. "I know him."

We'd lost our share of business to Serner over the years—every small agency had. When you do corporate work, you come across plenty of clients who want to use the biggest and best-known firm whether or not they'll do the best job, and the fact is that Serner did do a good job, so it's not even as though we could bad-mouth them with a clear conscience. And Bill Battles was a good investigator. He knew his way around every public record there was, and if you were looking to hire a mortgage trader he could tell you if the guy had ever been reprimanded back in summer camp.

But a corporate background check and a missing daughter are two very different things. There were people at Serner I'd go to if it were my daughter, and Bill Battles wasn't one of them.

Could another investigator have done a better job? Maybe. Could we have, if Mastaduno had come to us? And if we had, might Miranda have been alive today?

You could drive yourself crazy with questions like that. They'd gone to the top firm, the firm had assigned one of their top investigators, and Jocelyn Mastaduno had stayed missing. It happened.

I left a message on Bill's office voicemail asking him to call me. I tried to think of someone else I could call, but other than Big Murco, I was pretty well tapped out of phone numbers. I wanted to hear Susan's voice, know that she was okay, but there was no easy way to accomplish that. I considered stopping at the Derby after hours, but my side twinged at the thought.

There was only one other thing for me to do, and I'd been putting it off. I didn't relish going to Zen's even when I was in full health. But I needed to find out more about Khachadurian, and if the cops couldn't tell me anything useful, that left— Well, it left some people Leo wouldn't have been happy to see me talking to. And Zen's was where I would find them.

Chapter 9

Zen was Zenobia Salva, and her bar wasn't called Zen's except by the people who went there. Its official name was Dormicello, which was an in-joke of sorts, since Reuben Dormicello had been Zen's first husband, and he'd drunk himself to death. No one had ever seen Zen take a drink, but she worked the stick well enough to please her thirsty clientele. She'd have pleased her husband, too, if he'd lived to see it, but back when he was alive, she didn't own a bar yet, didn't own much of anything, in fact, except the clothes on her back, and she'd take those off readily enough if you had two hundred dollars you were willing to part with. I hadn't known her then, but I'd heard the story many times over the years from people at the bar, and if it wasn't quite the same any two times I heard it, Zen herself never seemed troubled by the inconsistencies. She had the impassive expression of someone who was beyond offending, though also the look of someone you didn't want to push too far.

The story had it that her second husband, who died of a knife wound in the laundry at Riker's Island while serving seven-to-ten for armed robbery, had won the bar in a poker game and willed it to her. The poker game part of the story sounded like a romantic embellishment to me, but who knows?

"You don't look so good," Zen said. She took a pull on a cigarette, laid it down on a saucer. "You getting enough sleep?"

"Probably not, but that's not the problem. Someone I used to know was killed the other day. I've been looking into it and getting nowhere, but someone must have thought I was getting somewhere, since they sent some muscle to teach me a lesson." I mimed a rabbit punch and got the slightest little shake of her head in response.

"You've got to take care of yourself, John."

"I'm still here, aren't I?" I said.

"You got any idea who you're dealing with?"

"Some. That's why I came here. Thought you might know someone who could help."

"You know," she said, "you can come by when you're not working on a case, too."

"I know."

She looked around the room. It wasn't packed yet, and it wouldn't be till later in the night, but already you could see the crowds forming. The ex-cons stayed near the walls, by themselves or in pairs, watching the doors and each other. The rummies sat at the bar nursing their drinks and telling old stories about great hauls they'd only pulled off in their imaginations. A few men clustered around the pool table, trading gibes and laying down bets on the ledge of the chalkboard. There were straight patrons, too, people who walked in off the street for a beer, ignoring the blacked-out windows and lack of a sign, but there weren't many and they generally got the feeling they weren't welcome pretty quickly. Though not always. Once, I remembered, a Wall Street power broker in striped tie and braces had gotten into a shoving match with a scrawny Puerto Rican kid named Simon Corrina. A smarter man would have seen the look in Corrina's eyes and stopped shoving, but then a smarter man would have taken the hint and stayed out of Zen's to begin with. Three of us were eventually able to pull Corrina off him, but then you can pry open the jaws of a bear trap, too.

How much blood had been spilled on the floor of this

bar, both before Zen took it over and since? I generally tried not to think about it, beyond the immediate problem of making sure none of mine was added to the tally.

"Tell me who you think it is," Zen said, "and I'll tell you if anyone here's likely to know anything."

"Murco Khachadurian," I said.

"Oh, Jesus. You sure can pick them. You talking about Big Murco or Little Murco?"

"Actually, I'm not sure. Whichever owns the Sin Factory."

Her eyes narrowed.

"It's a strip club—"

"I know it's a strip club. And your friend was a stripper, wasn't she? I seem to remember reading about some poor girl getting shot there. It was in the *Post*."

"*Daily News*, too. Page eighteen."

"And how did a college boy like you come to know a Sin Factory stripper?" She waved away her own question before I could answer it. "Forget I asked. You'd think I'd have learned to mind my own fucking business after all these years. You bring out the mother hen in me."

"It's okay," I said. "I knew her ten years ago, when we were in school together. She was going to be a doctor. An eye doctor. You know, treat glaucoma and prescribe glasses." Suddenly, I did feel tired, awfully tired. I was feeling the effects of the drink Leo had given me, and my bruises, and the night spent on the office couch, but even more than that, I was feeling the weight of the task I'd taken on, which was more than just finding Miranda's killer, it was finding Miranda herself, finding out who she had been, and how in God's name was I going to do that?

"The day before she was killed, she told someone she expected it to happen. She said she was afraid of Murco Khachadurian. It's the only lead I've got."

Zen bent forward, pointed to a table in the corner near the bathrooms. "See that guy there, the one with the forehead? Blue shirt, jeans. There." I saw who she meant. There was nothing special about his forehead except that you could see a lot of it, since his hairline had receded halfway up his scalp. The skin of his face showed the ravages of old acne scars, but otherwise he was a reasonably good-looking guy. "That's who you need to talk to."

He looked normal enough, and as Zen walked me over to him I found myself wondering what crimes he had committed. I imagine everyone else in the place was wondering the same thing about me.

When we got there, he looked from Zen to me and back again. "Yes?"

"This man's a friend of the house," Zen said. "He doesn't need to know your name, and you don't need to know his. I thought you could help each other out."

"What sort of help does he need?"

"I'm trying—"

"He's got a beef with Big Murco," Zen said. The man's eyebrows rose. "You see why I thought of you."

"What'd Murco do to you?" he asked me.

I lifted my shirt to show the bruise. "That, and killed a friend of mine."

"Let's talk," he said.

Zen brought over my glass and refilled his, but otherwise left us alone. The tables on either side of us were empty, and the noise from the pool table and the TV set and the bar masked our conversation pretty well, but he kept his voice low and so did I.

"What did Khachadurian do to you?" I asked.

He shook his head. "Let's talk about you."

How many times had I told the story? I was starting to

feel like the Ancient Mariner, buttonholing everyone with my tale of woe.

But what other way was there? I told him, told him about seeing Miranda in the paper, about going to the Sin Factory and getting thrown out, I told him about the bouncer and about what Miranda had said to Susan about Murco. I left Susan's name out of it—both her names. But the rest I told him.

"Your girlfriend was right," he said. "Murco does use the girls to move drugs. Not dime bags to the customers, nothing like that. He's a middleman, he'll take a few kilos and spread it out to three small dealers, maybe four, take a cut off the top. They're the ones who sell it to the street, and by then he's out of the picture." I knew better than to ask how he knew this. My money was on his being one of the three or four dealers—or more likely he had been one once and now Murco had cut him out. "A ditch in Jersey City I don't know about, but he certainly wouldn't let one of the girls get too talkative. Your girlfriend had a mouth on her?"

Did she? When I'd known her, she'd been pretty shy. But people change. I shrugged.

"Murco's certainly got a temper, and you wouldn't want to get on his bad side."

I rubbed my side. "Tell me about it," I said.

"That? That's nothing. You heard about the burglary, right?"

"No."

"You should have been here last week."

"What happened last week?"

"Got to go back to the beginning. Maybe six weeks ago, these two guys break into Murco's house. The man lives in Scarsdale. A house that's like two mansions side by side, and he lives out there by himself—no staff, nothing, not since the son moved out and his wife died. So, these two punks are going through the neighborhood, and they come to this enormous place, and they figure, this guy's got to have some good stuff. So they break in through the garage, go room to room, filling up their bags. And God knows he's got plenty to take any night of the week—but just as it happens, this particular night is the night before Murco is going to be making a buy, so he has a suitcase full of cash waiting to be handed over to the gentlemen from Colombia. The punks go into his bedroom, and there he is, counting the money. They must've thought they'd died and gone to heaven.

"They pull guns on him, tie him up, smack him around some, take the money, and they leave. A million dollars in cash, plus whatever else they picked up along the way. It's a better score than they could've imagined. There's just one problem."

"What's that?"

"They didn't kill him." He finished the rest of his drink, set the glass down carefully. "I could have told them. You're going to pull something like that, you have to go all the way. You can't leave him there tied up, blood running down his face, for his son to find when the old man doesn't call for two days. I don't care if you wore masks, disguised your voices, I don't care if you left no fingerprints, this man's not the fucking police force, he'll find you and then you're going to wish you'd never been born. And that's what happened."

I felt my skin start to crawl.

"Last week, it must have been the day after Christmas, the son came in here. Little Murco, though you just try to call him that to his face. He calls himself 'Catch.' "

I remembered Roy's question the first time I met him.

Have you seen the big guy here tonight? I'd asked, and he'd said, *Catch?*

"Anyway, Catch comes in, and he sits down over there, by the phone, and he's carrying a dice cup, rattling it like a guy on the street with a cup of change. We'd all heard about what had happened, and you could tell he wanted someone to ask him about it, but no one says a word to him. So he goes to the bar and says to Zen, but loud so everyone can hear, 'You know those guys that broke into my father's place? You won't be seeing them any more.' And he spills out the dice cup all over the bar, and what it was full of is teeth. He spills them out, spreads them around a little with one finger, then he walks out."

"Lovely," I said.

"Now, I can't tell you for sure whose teeth those were, and neither can anyone else, since Zen did the right thing and got rid of them. But I'd bet dollars to doughnuts Big Murco got his million back, and those two poor bastards are in a landfill somewhere, gumming their food in the next life."

"Murco do this sort of thing a lot?"

"He doesn't have to. You do it once, people tend to leave you alone after that."

"The cops think he's small potatoes," I said.

"He is. He's just a vicious small potato."

"And Miranda? What are people saying about her murder?"

"People figure Murco probably did it, but then again, it didn't really have a lot of style to it, just—" He made a gun of his forefinger and thumb, fired it at me twice.

"No teeth in a dice cup, you mean."

"The man does like to send a message."

I nodded. "And why are you telling me all this?"

"You're a friend of Zen's," he said, "and Murco's no friend of mine."

On my way out, Zen called me over. "Was he able to help you?"

"You didn't tell me about the teeth," I said.

"I didn't want to scare you."

"Yes you did, you just wanted someone else to do the dirty work for you."

"If I'd said you should lay off, would you have listened to me?"

"No," I said.

"But you're going to, right?" She looked in my eyes, saw something there she didn't like.

I patted her on the arm. "Give my molars to Leo," I said. "You can hang the bicuspids over the bar."

Chapter 10

Bill Battles called me back in the morning and agreed to meet me at his office. He said he'd have to verify with Mastaduno that it was okay to share information with me, and I told him to be my guest. By the time I arrived, he apparently had, since he greeted me by dropping five pounds of files in my lap. Then he pulled open the blinds to let some light in and offered me a cup of coffee.

It reminded me of what I was missing out on working for Leo. Serner's offices filled the top three floors of an office building on Madison and Fifty-ninth, and Bill's office filled one corner of the middle floor. He wasn't quite their top producer, I guess, or maybe it was just that he wasn't a corporate officer—one way or another he'd been denied the top floor—but even one of Serner's second-tier corner offices was light years away from the ground-floor suite Leo and I shared in Chelsea. Bill's windows looked out over the avenue, and we were high enough up that you could look down on the traffic and not hear a sound. If you stood at the right angle, you could see the spires of St. Patrick's Cathedral in the distance. In our office, if you stood at the right angle near the window, you could see into the kitchen of an Indian restaurant.

I accepted the coffee, burned my tongue on it, and set it aside. I opened the first file. There was a picture clipped to the inside of the folder showing a pair of college-age girls in Rianon sweatshirts and blue jeans, one with her hip cocked and arms crossed, the other with her arm around the first girl's waist and her head resting on the first girl's shoulder. I looked hard at the pair. The one on the left was the subject of the five pounds of reports that followed. The one on the right was Miranda.

Miranda hadn't changed much by the time this picture was taken. She looked a little thinner, maybe, but the yearbook photo had only been a headshot, and my ten-year-old memories were, as Leo had pointed out, not entirely reliable. She'd given up glasses somewhere along the way, presumably for contacts.

Jocelyn Mastaduno was a tiny bit taller than Miranda, a little heavier. She had shorter hair and, if you could go by their poses in this one photo, a cockier attitude. They looked like sisters. It wasn't even a matter of resemblance as much as it was something about the way they were standing, the way Miranda held onto Jocelyn's waist, the look of contentment on her face as she rested on Jocelyn's shoulder. It had the intimacy of a family photo.

"One of the other girls in her class took that," Bill said. "Katherine Chin, I think."

"I talked to her. She's married, living in Chicago now. Katherine Lewis."

"Good to know. I'll get her number from you if we need to do a follow-up."

I turned the pages, not reading anything in detail but getting a feel for the work Serner had done, who they had talked to. Professors, students, area residents. The one travel agent in town, who said she hadn't made any arrangements at either girl's request. Local police. The school newspaper and the local newspaper. Then branching further out: people in neighboring towns, people who'd known the girls before college. It was very thorough. In a way, I was surprised they hadn't called me. But the investigation had mainly focused on Jocelyn, as was appropriate given that her father was paying the bills.

Jocelyn also seemed to have been the instigator behind whatever the two of them did. Students who knew them had told Serner that Miranda had dropped out of Intro to Psych a week after Jocelyn had, that she had signed up for classes in yoga and modern dance when Jocelyn had, that Jocelyn had been the one behind their request to room together in Heward Hall. It didn't quite make Miranda out to be a doe-eyed follower and Jocelyn some sort of Svengali, but Jocelyn had tended to dominate in the relationship.

And what sort of relationship had it been? Some of the girls' peers hadn't hesitated to speculate. Neither Miranda nor Jocelyn seemed to date much or to date any one boy for long. They preferred spending time together. It wouldn't have been the first fling between two girls on the Rianon campus, and it's not surprising that some people drew that conclusion. But as far as Serner could find, there was no evidence one way or the other.

I set the first file aside and started flipping through the second. There was more material here than I could read sitting in Bill's office, and I asked him whether there was a conference room I could use.

"There is," he said, "but you don't have to do that. Those are all copies, except for the photo, which we'll need to keep here. Sign them out and you can take them back to your office."

"Leo'll think you're coming after me again if he sees your files on my desk."

"Let him think it," Bill said. "Maybe he'll give you a raise."

I shook my head. "He's paying me what he can."

"I hope you realize you're too good to be wasted in a little two-man operation like that."

"If I didn't know better, I'd say you *were* coming after me again."

"I'm just saying."

"Listen," I said, "I didn't see anything here about Miranda's dancing in any of the local strip clubs. I don't know when she started, but I was assuming it was around the time her mother died, which would have been before she left school. Do you know if anyone mentioned anything along those lines?"

"It's not a question we asked."

"Yeah, well, why would you? All I'm saying is, she must have started sometime. Am I going to find anything about it in here?"

"No," he said. "Believe me, if we'd heard a breath of it, we would have followed up on it."

It was disappointing, but not a surprise.

"Still, maybe you'll find something useful in there."
He handed me their form non-disclosure agreement, and
I signed it. "God knows we never did."

We were lying on her bed, in the apartment on Eighty-
fourth Street, the one that was now home to the Bakers
and next door to a youth center instead of a synagogue.
Her mother was at work, and would be for two hours still,
which was plenty of time to finish our math homework,
or would have been if we could keep our hands off each
other. She'd just discovered what it did to me when she
put her tongue in my ear, and so had I, and both of us
liked it more than trigonometry. Her shirt and bra were
on the floor, on top of my shirt, which had come off first,
and her skirt and my pants were crumpled next to us in
the bed. But she still had her panties on and I still wore
my Fruit of the Loom briefs, and we both understood it
would stay that way throughout, one last concession to
the pointless, old-fashioned rules we'd set for ourselves.

It hardly mattered. We couldn't have enjoyed ourselves more if we'd gone further, and now, thinking back
on it, I remembered that afternoon more fondly than any
of the encounters I'd had later, first at NYU and then,
after graduating, with girls I met through friends or at
parties. There had been women since Miranda—but
none I'd loved, not even for a night.

We lay in her bed, my fingers tracing the line of her sex
through her underwear, and she told me about Rianon
College, with its ophthalmology-focused pre-med program, one of the oldest in the country, and its campus, so
green and open, so different from anything we'd ever
known in New York City. They'd accepted her on an Early
Decision basis, she said, which meant that for her the college application process was now over. What about me?

What about me.

Thinking back now, I could remember the bed, I could remember the feel of her body under my hand, I could even remember the quality of the light filtering in through her bedroom window, motes of dust dancing slowly over our heads. But I couldn't remember my answer. I'd known I'd never leave the city, I'd known that since I was a kid—I couldn't imagine living anywhere else. But I wouldn't have told her that, not then. Did I join her in spinning a dream of going away to New Mexico, cutting all our ties to our friends and our homes? Did I tell her I'd go with her, that I'd apply, too, maybe for the program in literature, or history, or God only knows what? And if I did, was it a lie, or did I mean it— maybe only for that afternoon, maybe only for that minute, but with all my heart?

She'd gone. I'd stayed. But all through the years that followed, part of me had gone with her, vicariously enjoying the rolling, green campus when I was riding crammed subways past Washington Square, living with her in a clean suburb when my real life took place in a fourth-story walk-up with windows that didn't close properly and junkies outside on the sidewalk. Leo was my real life. While she was learning to heal people, he was training me to uncover the worst things about them. But late at night, in bed with the door closed and the blinds drawn and my eyes shut, I'd see through her eyes, and because she was someplace better, so was I.

Only now I knew she wasn't, that she hadn't been any-where better. Everything I'd imagined for her—the hap-piness, the comfortable life—those were the lie. Somehow she'd fallen into my world.

Chapter 11

There were more than four hundred pages of interviews, and I read them all. Everyone had something to say, and everyone had nothing to say. Jocelyn was a girl like any other, a solid B student who showed no signs of caring about her classes, an unremarkable participant in campus events, and more often than not Miranda was at her side. Then they were gone, and no one missed them for long.

Were there any hints before they left that either girl might be unhappy? You wouldn't know it from the file. Had they ever gotten in any sort of trouble? Not so as you'd notice. Why would they leave school? The answer Serner had received was a collective shrug.

Had they gone off to Canada, as someone had suggested to me? It was one of two possibilities, the other being that they had gone somewhere else.

I thought about ways I might turn up more information, but none seemed promising—Serner would have tried them, and I wasn't likely to do better with them after seven years had passed. More promising, it seemed to me, was the idea of working backwards. After all, the one thing I had to work with that Serner hadn't had is that I knew where the story ended, or at least where half of it did. I knew where Miranda had ended up.

I tried to imagine the two of them, as close as sisters or maybe closer, when the news arrived that Miranda's mother had died. Jocelyn was at best a decent student and only lightly committed to school. Miranda had cared a great deal about her studies once, but her grades had turned out poor, and maybe she'd felt the dream of medical school slipping away from her anyway. Then the telegram comes, or the phone call, and suddenly she has no family anymore and no source of money. Maybe Jocelyn has been working on her to drop out anyway, and this gives her the final push to do it.

Maybe. It was a plausible picture. But it was still a long way from stripping at the Sin Factory.

They need money—for tuition or just to live, and either Miranda's inheritance doesn't supply enough or it would take too long to come, or both. Maybe Jocelyn could get some from her parents, but she's already not talking to her parents much, and anyway it's one thing to support your daughter, another thing to support her roommate—especially if maybe she's more than just a roommate. They've been taking modern dance and yoga; they're free, attractive, and twenty years old; and one day someone tells them about a club, one a town or two over, where no one who knows them ever goes. Or maybe they come across a club during a weekend driving trip and laughingly dare each other to go inside. Maybe it's amateur night, a quick fifty dollars for any good-looking girl willing to get up on stage and take off her shirt.

Maybe. Maybe the first time it just pays for their gas and their drinks, but the second time it pays for their books and their medical insurance, and before long they're pulling down four hundred, five hundred a week and the only cost is that dancing to loud music at two in the morning means being too tired to take tests the next day. Maybe they want to get away for a while, so they put in for a leave of absence, pack the contents of their dorm room into a car, and hit the road, paying as they go with this new currency they've discovered. There isn't a town in America of any reasonable size that doesn't have at least a couple of strip clubs, on the outskirts if not in the town proper, and maybe it starts out as a big, liberated adventure before settling, at some point along the way, into being a grind.

Because it must have. Not just because taking your clothes off for money in front of rooms full of rowdy drunks must lose its charm awfully quickly, even if you've got a friend along for the ride, but also because we knew that somewhere along the way the friends had split up. They may have been a sister act in New Mexico, but Miranda was working solo by the time she got to New York.

Or did I know that? No—the truth was, I didn't know any of this. Maybe they were still together when she arrived in New York and only split up later. Maybe the stripping didn't start right out of Rianon and only began when the cash ran out along the road. All sorts of scenarios were possible. But as I thought through them one by one, a picture began to emerge. Anything was possible, but some things were more likely than others. Initially, for instance, I'd been thinking only of Miranda as having turned to stripping, but the more I thought about it, the more I realized this wasn't the way it must have happened. Miranda had followed Jocelyn's lead in so many things—she wouldn't have been the one to initiate this.

And that gave me a thread to pull on. Two college girls working their way east starting in 1996, two twenty-year-old, Rianon-educated blondes coming to work at the same clubs at the same time, if not outright working in tandem—that was the sort of thing people might remember even seven years later.

Assuming I could get the right people on the phone. Now the question was, who did I know with contacts in the strip club business? There was Wayne Lenz, but I didn't see him doing me any favors. There was Murco Khachadurian.

And then there was Susan.

My friend was behind the bar again at the Derby. Maybe he did own the place, or maybe he just liked working lots of hours. He eyed me with a certain amount of suspicion that he made no effort to disguise.

"She's not here," he said.

"I didn't think she would be. But I told her that if I needed to get in touch with her, I'd leave a message with you."

"I know," he said. "She checked yesterday to see if you'd left one."

"She look okay?"

"Why do you ask?"

"I just want to know she's okay."

"No sign she wasn't," he said.

"No need to jump down my throat," I said.

"Young man, I don't like you hanging around here. I told you that the last time I saw you, and I meant it."

Young man. No one had called me that for a while.

"I wasn't planning to hang around. I'd just been planning to ask you to tell her I'd been by. But maybe I should. If she came by yesterday, she'll probably come again today."

"If you're going to hang around, it's not going to be in my bar. You can do what you like on the street."

"I'll pay for my drinks," I said.

"Not here you won't, because you won't be served any."

We stared each other down for a bit while I got my temper under control. This wasn't Zen's, but it's never good to get into shoving matches, especially when you can't see the other man's hands. Somewhere along the way, Keegan's had dropped behind the bar.

"Fine," I said. "I'll wait outside."

"That's your privilege."

I stepped out into the street, buttoned my jacket collar against the cold. I wished I'd brought gloves, but I hadn't thought of it. I stuck my hands in my pockets instead.

Through the window, I saw Keegan—if that's who he was—watching me. He lifted a phone receiver from the wall behind him, dialed a number, and after a moment started talking. He didn't take his eyes off me.

Who was he calling? It only hit me after a minute, and then I couldn't believe how stupid I'd been. Who would he be calling? How many people would have an interest in knowing that some man was hanging around bothering the Sin Factory girls? Maybe Keegan did keep his place open nights out of a feeling of paternal kindness toward the girls; on the other hand, maybe it was an arrangement he had with the club's management. Either way, he'd be bound to have some sort of relationship with Lenz. More of one, at least, than he had with me.

And that answered a question that should have been bothering me but hadn't been: How had Roy known where to find me the night he'd given me his "warning"? Someone must have tipped him or Lenz off when I left the Derby, and watching Keegan on the phone now, I didn't have much doubt as to who it had been.

Which made walking away the smart thing for me to do now. But there was a problem with that. If Keegan had told Lenz he'd seen me talking to Susan, she might be in danger, too. And even if she wasn't, I needed to talk to her, and leaving messages at the bar was no longer an option.

It was a few minutes to six, but there was no way of knowing when she would come by today, or even whether she would. The only person I could be confident would be showing up soon was the man who'd come close to putting me in the hospital two days ago.

It was already as dark as the night would get, but it was still close to rush hour, so the street was full. Cars were jostling to beat each other to the next red light, and the pedestrians on the sidewalk were doing the equivalent.

But there were lulls in the flow of the crowd, and during one of them I spotted Roy. He was coming casually from the direction of the club, wearing a duster-style leather overcoat over corduroys and a tan shirt. He'd been smarter than I had: he'd remembered his gloves.

When he was half a block away, he saw me standing in front of the Derby. He didn't walk any faster, or for that matter any slower.

I looked back over my shoulder, and almost missed her—but then I realized who the woman was with her hand on Keegan's door and one foot inside the bar.

"Susan." I grabbed her arm and steered her away from the bar. Now, when I glanced back over my shoulder, Roy seemed to be moving faster. "Come with me."

"What's going on?"

"I'll tell you later, just keep moving."

"John!" She pushed my hand off her arm and stopped dead. "What's going on?"

I started to say something, but it was too late. Roy was pushing through the last of the crowd separating us from him. We wouldn't be able to outrun him—and if we tried, if Susan turned and ran with me, it would be the same as announcing she was on my side against them.

"Yell at me," I whispered.

"What?" she said.

"I grabbed you. Just do it."

Then Roy was beside us.

Chapter 12

"Get your fucking hands off me," Susan said.

"This guy bothering you?" Roy said. He took hold of my arm.

"I'm trying to go in, he grabs me."

"We've had trouble with him before," Roy said. He turned to me. "Haven't we?"

What the hell was I doing? I couldn't take another beating. And that was assuming a beating was all Roy had in mind this time. "No," I said, "there's no trouble."

"So why're you pawing the ladies, man? You can't do that." His grip tightened, and even through the padding of his glove and my coat, it hurt. "We're going to need to have a little talk."

"It was a mistake," I said. "I thought she was someone else." I winced as he squeezed harder. Over his shoulder, I saw Susan's face go pale. She started going through her purse.

"Sure it was," Roy said. "Like it was a mistake when you bothered her two nights ago. You make a lot of mistakes, man."

"It won't happen again."

"Now that's the truth," Roy said. "My boss told me to make sure it doesn't."

"What are you going to do," I said, "hit me out here in front of all these people?"

"No," he said, steering me back toward the club, "we're going to show you a good time in one of our private rooms tonight."

I couldn't let him get me inside—if he did, I might never come out again. But I had a couple of blocks to deal with that. The important thing was getting him away from Susan. I let him walk me down the block.

Suddenly he stopped, and I saw a hand between us reaching up to tap him on the shoulder. We both turned back, and Susan was there, holding a canister in her hand, about the size of a cologne bottle or a travel-sized can of shaving cream. With her thumb, she depressed the trigger on top.

I dodged to one side and he tried to dodge to the other, but she followed him with the can, spraying into his eyes with a cloud of pepper spray that made me wince even from two feet away. Roy screamed, tried to wipe the stuff out of his eyes. With his other arm he was waving blindly in front of him, trying to knock the can away. Susan kept spraying, even once it was useless, just hitting the back of his sleeve. I took her arm and ran out into traffic with her, dodging cars, holding up my hand to get others to stop. One driver after another started honking.

"You shouldn't have done that," I said, pulling her along.

We were on the other side now, and Roy was still clutching at his eyes down the block from the Derby, cursing, with a crowd gathered around him at a distance of a few feet. Some of the people were pointing at us, and one seemed to be running to find a policeman.

"We need to get out of here," I said. "Come on."

We ran toward Twenty-third Street, turned in and

raced to the subway station. My side was aching again and I was out of breath. At the turnstile, I fished in my pocket and she fished in her purse. I found my MetroCard and slid it through the readers of two turnstiles. "Go. Go!"

We pushed through to the platform. Behind us we could still hear noises from the street, shouting, cars honking. A train rumbled into the station and we got on it without even checking what train it was. It was going somewhere, and anywhere was better than here.

Miraculously, there were two empty seats together. I collapsed into one of them. She sat in the other and put her face in her hands.

"You shouldn't have done it, Susan," I said.

She raised her head and I saw that she was crying. "What should I have done? Let him take you away?"

"I would have gotten away from him. Somehow."

"I can never go back there now."

"No, probably not. Not there."

"You think anyone else will hire me? They all talk to each other."

She put her face back in her hands.

We'd gotten on a downtown train, which was fine if we wanted to go to the Village or Soho or Chinatown. But where did we want to go? I didn't know where she lived, assuming she lived in the city at all—it had sounded like she was on some sort of circuit, traveling from club to club, and for all I knew her permanent home was in some other part of the country entirely. We could go to my apartment or my office, but neither of those seemed especially safe right now—where I worked was no secret, and though my home number was unlisted, it wouldn't take much effort to turn up my address. We needed a place where she could crash and where we'd be sure no one would look for her.

There weren't too many choices. Leo commuted in from a one-bedroom in Jersey, and I wasn't going to drag her out there. We could take a hotel room, but I didn't have enough cash on me, and charging a room to a credit card with my name on it—or hers—didn't seem too smart. I could only think of one other place in the city that no one knew about or would connect with me, a place where I could stow her and she'd be safe, a spare bedroom I knew about because I'd lived there once, years ago.

I could take her home to mother.

When had I seen my mother last? It had been months. Her disappointment in me showed in her face, but she was much too polite to say anything, especially in front of a guest. I introduced Susan as Rachel, and had a strange feeling as I watched them shake hands. *Mom, this is Rachel. She's a stripper on the run from a thug she blinded with pepper spray and his boss, who works for a drug dealer who may also be a murderer. Can she stay here with you under a false name?*

"How long have you known each other?" my mother asked. Before either of us could answer, she said, "I'm sorry, where are my manners? Would you like some tea? I know John doesn't drink tea, but would you like some?"

Susan shook her head.

"Some juice? Coffee? I don't have any soft drinks, I'm afraid."

In a small voice, Susan said, "I'm fine, thanks."

"Well, all right." Now my mother waited for the answer to her first question.

"Rachel is involved with a case I'm working on," I said.

"We only met a few days ago."

"All right," she said again, slowly. "I just thought, if you're bringing her to meet me—"

"I'm not—it's just that she's got no place to go." On the way down, Susan had confirmed that she'd been staying at a hotel, and that the staff at the Sin Factory knew which hotel it was. "There are problems at the place she's working, and she can't go back there or go home, and I was thinking she could stay here for a few days."

"Well, of course, John, you know that's still your room and you can use it any time you want." That was what she said. What she meant was, *but I never expected you to show up out of the blue and put a strange woman in it. You and I are going to need to have a talk about this later, when we're alone.*

"Mom, you remember Miranda Sugarman?" Her face lit up. She'd always liked Miranda, had made no secret of her hope that we'd eventually get married. I put my hand on her arm and stroked it gently. "Miranda was shot a few days ago. She's dead."

"Oh my God."

"Rachel worked with Miranda at the place where it happened, and she's not safe there. I'm trying to help her. Do you understand?"

"Yes. Yes, of course." It was as if a curtain had dropped, and my mother suddenly looked her age. She'd turn sixty-one in a few weeks, and though I didn't like to think of her that way, she was starting to look more like an old woman each time I saw her. Her hair had gone grey when I was a kid, but while I was living there she'd had it dyed every other week. No more. Her face was narrower than it had been, her nose sharper. And though she stood as straight as ever, the top of her head only came up to my shoulder now.

"I should call Barbara," she said, and stood up to head to the phone.

"I'm sorry, Mom. I went there, and Barbara's—" Was there a good way to say it? They hadn't been close, but they'd talked from time to time, no doubt conspired about the grandchildren we'd give them. "They told me she had a heart attack seven years ago."

My mother sat down again. "Everyone's going," she said quietly. "Every day, you turn on the news and it's someone else. Last week it was that actor, the one from all the westerns."

"Michael Tynant," I said. "I saw that."

"You know who else died? Elyse Knechtel. Right here, 14-D, you remember. Just the other day, they found her in her bed, like she was asleep."

"I'm sorry," I said.

"And you know who else? Maria, who used to run the bakery on Seventh Street? Her daughter. She was only twenty-nine. Your age. Some sort of disease, muscular something. Everybody's dying." She looked at Susan, who'd been standing silently by the door, watching us. Susan's eyes were red and her hands were shaking. "Listen to me, talking about things like this. Of course you can stay here, sweetheart. Let me get you some sheets and a towel."

We sat in my old room, I on the room's one chair, Susan on the twin bed with its fresh sheets. My *Reservoir Dogs* poster was still on the wall and I was sure none of the old clothing I'd left in the closet when I'd moved out had been touched.

"So, what happens now?" Susan asked. She sounded numb, dazed. I couldn't blame her.

"You stay here for a few days while we sort everything

out," I said. "First thing is you give me your hotel key and we get your things out of your room and bring them back here."

"You can't go there."

"No, but my boss can. They've never seen him, and even if they're watching the hotel, they wouldn't know what room you're in."

"Unless someone at the front desk told them."

"If there's anyone watching the room, Leo won't go in. He knows what he's doing."

"What if they're waiting inside the room?"

"He's an ex-cop, Susan. He can take care of himself better than either of us."

"Okay."

"Next, I'm going to need your help. I need to know how Miranda ended up at the Sin Factory. You know people in this business. I want you to make some calls for me." I explained my theory about how Miranda and Jocelyn had gotten started, gave her the timeframe and the geography, and asked her to find out anything she could. "Where did they work, what did they do, when were they there—anything."

"I'll help if I can," she said, "but I'm not sure I'll be able to find anything."

"I think you will."

"I've worked in a lot of clubs," she said, "but there have got to be ten times as many that I've never heard of."

"You probably know people who know them." She looked uncertain. "You know more than I do, anyway. Please. Just do the best you can. It's important."

"All right," she said. "And what will you be doing while I'm calling all the strip clubs in America and your partner is breaking into my hotel room?"

"I'll be talking to Murco Khachadurian," I said.

Chapter 13

I called Leo from the hallway outside my mother's apartment. It was after seven and normally he'd be heading to Port Authority soon to catch the 7:47 bus back home, but there was another bus at 9:40, and if he missed that there was a train. I explained what I needed him to do and told him I'd be at the office in twenty minutes to give him the key.

"Every day I seem to be getting more involved in this project of yours," he said. "Don't I remember you telling me when all this started that you didn't need my help?"

"I didn't say I didn't need it. I said I wasn't asking for it."

"And now you're asking?"

"It'll take you twenty minutes. Not even. Fifteen." He didn't say anything. "Yes, I'm asking."

"Should I take a gun?" he said.

"It's just picking up a couple of bags from a hotel room."

He thought about it. "I'll take a gun," he said. "You probably should, too."

I didn't much like carrying a gun, but there were times when it was called for. "Yes. I probably should."

I pushed the button for the elevator, and while I was waiting, a woman came out of 14-D carrying an armload of cardboard hatboxes. She looked a little like Mrs. Knechtel, thin brown hair framing an oval face seamed with tiny wrinkles. A sister, I guessed, or maybe a close cousin. She tried to push the door to the garbage room open with her hip. I opened it for her and held it while she lowered the boxes to the floor. Two framed posters were already there, leaning against the wall.

"I heard what happened," I said. "I'm sorry."

"It's just so sudden," she said. "And there are so many things to go through. I don't know where to start."

I knew how she felt.

We traded, the key for the gun, and then each headed off in our own direction: Leo to the Martinique on Broadway and Thirty-second, I to my apartment. I watched him through the back window of my cab, saw him with his arm raised to hail one of his own. In the midwinter darkness, in his heavy overcoat and wool cap, Leo suddenly looked old to me, too.

There was no one walking in the street as we pulled up to my building, and just a few cars were parked at the curb. The front door was glass and the hallway beyond was well lit. I could see all the way in to the stairs, and there was no one there. But there were plenty of places someone could stand and not be visible. Behind the door leading down to the basement was one choice; the second, third, or fourth floor landings were others. And there was always inside my apartment itself. I'd installed a Medeco lock and a police bar, but neither was a guarantee against intruders, especially when the building's windows were so insecure.

I thought about going around to the back, up the fire escape, and in through the window myself, but apart from the noise it would have made and the fact that anyone in my apartment would have a clear shot at me long before I'd have one at him, I just didn't have it in me tonight.

I gripped the gun in my right hand inside my jacket pocket and readied the front door key in my left. No one came while I was opening the door or, once I was in the vestibule next to the mailboxes, while I waited for it to swing closed. No one stopped me on the stairs. No one fired down on me from above or came up behind me from below. I took each flight slowly, pausing at each landing to release my grip on the gun, wipe my palm, and re-grip. The stairwell was silent, aside from the muffled sounds of television coming from behind some apartment doors.

When I got to the fourth floor, I listened at my door for a full minute before unlocking it and cautiously pushing it open with my foot. I had the gun out, held before me in both hands to steady my aim if I needed it. I let the door slam shut behind me and quickly turned left and right to look into the kitchen and the bathroom. No one was standing behind the shower curtain or behind the kitchen door. There wasn't room for anyone in the apartment's one closet, but I checked anyway. I turned in a circle, trying to spot anything that looked like it had been disturbed. Nothing did. I lowered the gun, went back to the front door and locked it.

Murco Khachadurian's number was where I'd left it, next to the piece of paper with Kirsch's and Mastaduno's. I slipped both pieces of paper into my pocket along with whatever cash I had in my desk drawer. I unplugged the cell phone charger from the wall, coiled up the cord and put the whole thing in my jacket pocket. No way of knowing when I'd be back here next. What else might I need? I looked around. The Serner files were still lying on the bed. I slipped the rubber band back over them and put them under the bed. Not much of a hiding place, but it also wasn't the end of the world if they got stolen.

What else? I could change my clothes. I could take another hot shower. I could try to get some sleep, start with a fresh head tomorrow. These were all reasonable

things to do, and they were all just excuses to put off what
I had to do.

I dug out the cell phone number and dialed it.

His voice, when it finally came, sounded hoarse, like he'd
spent the night talking in a crowded bar or the past
twenty years smoking two packs a day.

"Hello, who is this?"

"Mr. Khachadurian?"

"Yes? Who is this?"

"My name is John Blake," I said. "I'm a private investigator."

"*Blake?* You're calling me? How did you get this
number?"

"It sounds like you know who I am," I said. "That
means you probably know I'm looking into the death of
Miranda Sugarman."

Silence. Then: "I can't talk to you now. I'm with company. I'll call you back."

"Why don't you tell them it's a personal call and you
have to take it," I said.

"Don't push me," he said. "We'll talk when I'm ready
to talk." The line was disconnected.

I put the cell phone down on my desk and watched it.
Like the proverbial pot, it didn't boil. But that was the
number Khachadurian would be calling on if he did call
back, since that was the number that would have shown
up on his phone's display.

I wondered what he was doing. Company, he'd said,
and in the background there'd been the noise of conver-
sations, the sound of cutlery and dishes. It could have
been a dinner party in Scarsdale or a restaurant just
down the block. No way to tell.

He'd known my name. Of course, all that meant is that

Lenz had told him about the incident at the club, or maybe that one of the cards I'd handed out to the girls had made it back to him—but all the same it made me anxious. I had the feeling that Murco Khachadurian had been paying closer attention to me than I had realized.

The more time passed without his calling back, the more nervous I got. What if he did know where I lived? It was certainly possible. That risk was why I hadn't brought Susan here, and it was a good reason for me not to stick around either. Maybe there hadn't been someone waiting for me in my apartment, but that didn't mean there wasn't someone watching the building from the street, or that there wouldn't be momentarily.

I grabbed the cell phone and the gun, took one last look around for anything I might be forgetting. I was locking the door behind me when the cell phone started buzzing. I pocketed my keys and flipped the phone open left-handed, holding tight to the gun in my other hand.

"I ended my dinner early for you, Mr. Blake," he said. "Now I'm ready to talk."

"Good." I started down the stairs.

"I want to know everything you know about Miranda Sugarman," he said.

"That's funny," I said, "I was about to say exactly the same thing."

"Well, then, maybe we can sit down together, share some information."

"I appreciate the invitation, but I prefer the phone. Scarsdale is a little out of my way."

"Who said anything about Scarsdale? We're right here, Mr. Blake."

I rounded the corner to the last half-flight of stairs. An enormous man was standing with one foot on the lowest step and a gun held casually in his fist. Behind him, a thin man with a grey crew cut was talking into a cell phone. He saw me and flipped it closed, raised the gun in his other hand. "Put your gun down, Mr. Blake. And the phone. You won't need them."

Chapter 14

Maybe in his prime Leo would have gone for the double play. Or maybe he would have turned around and run for it, back up the four floors and into the apartment, or maybe up five and out onto the roof. And maybe he'd have pulled it off. I didn't have a chance.

I lowered the gun, put it down on the stairs, snapped my cell phone back into its holster.

The younger man came up to meet me, leaned over to snatch up my gun, and gestured me down to the foot of the stairs. He stood well over six feet and had a neck like a linebacker's packed into a collarless shirt. It looked like he used the same grease in his hair that Lenz used. This must be Little Murco, though it had clearly been years since the nickname had fit.

Big Murco was a head shorter than his son but had the same olive coloring and a skinnier version of the same features. He looked a little like Jack Kevorkian, I thought. He held the front door open and his son prodded me in the back with his pistol. I stepped outside.

Across the street, a black four-door sedan sat with its engine running and its lights on. Had it been there before, waiting for me when I'd gotten home? I couldn't remember. Most likely Little Murco—Catch—had been watching the building, maybe with instructions to call his dad when I showed up. Then I'd thrown a monkey wrench into things by calling him myself. If I hadn't, would they have just kept watching, hoping I'd lead them to something—maybe to Susan—or would they eventually have come calling on me? I'd never know now.

"Where are we going?" I asked as the father followed me into the car's back seat. Catch squeezed in behind the steering wheel.

"Nowhere. We're just going to sit and talk. And you're going to tell me what you've found out about that bitch who set me up."

I thought back to the conversation I'd had at Zen's. "You don't mean the burglary, do you? I thought you got the guys who did that."

"You see? This is a man who knows how to do his job." He said this to his son, who was turned sideways in his seat and watching over the headrest, gun at the ready. "Yes, I mean the burglary." He pointed to a scar running from above his right eye to his hairline. It looked recent and was about the right size to have been made with the butt of a pistol. "It's true that I got the men who did this to me. I could show you more of what they did, but I won't. Let's just say those two men won't be doing it to anyone else ever again."

"So?"

"Those two men—they were nothing. Amateurs. They didn't plan the job themselves. Someone else told them where to go and what to do and when to do it. It was no accident that they broke in when they did. Someone knew I'd have a lot of cash at home that night. Someone who got half the take for putting the finger on me. Someone who walked away with five hundred thousand dollars of my money."

"You think it was Miranda?"

"I know it was."

"Why?"

"Because," he rasped, "they told me it was. While they could still talk."

I thought about Catch and the cup full of teeth. I pictured the two burglars tied to chairs, the father and son working them over till they spilled everything they knew. I looked from one to the other. Would the old man have held their heads, or would he have been the one working the pliers?

"It doesn't make sense," I said. "How could Miranda have known about the money?"

"I don't know, Mr. Blake. But I can tell when a man's lying and when he's telling the truth, and those two, at the end . . . they weren't lying."

No, they probably wouldn't have been—and it didn't sound as though Murco was, either. He believed what they'd told him, and he believed what he was telling me. But what did that mean? If it was true, it meant Miranda hadn't just turned into a stripper—she'd turned into a thief as well. It also meant he'd had one hell of a reason to kill her. It certainly explained why Miranda had been so frightened of him.

But if he had killed her, why was he talking to me now? "You killed Miranda," I said, "and now you can't find the money she took from you."

"If I'd killed her, Mr. Blake, you'd better believe I'd have gotten her to tell me where the money was first."

"You're saying you didn't kill her?"

"Of course I am."

"You realize everyone thinks you did it."

"Everyone's an idiot. You think I would have done it in

my own club? You think I would have left the body there for Lenz to find? You think I'm stupid?"

It didn't seem to call for an answer.

For the first time, Catch spoke. His voice was a husky baritone. "If we'd killed her," he said, "it wouldn't have been with two bullets to the back of the head either." His eyes were completely dead. This was the man who'd held the pliers, I decided.

"Don't get me wrong," the father said, "I would have killed her, if I'd known she was the one who set me up. But I didn't know it was Sugarman until after she was dead."

"You said the two men you caught told you—"

"They told us the person who'd set them up for the job was a woman, a stripper named Jessie they'd met at a club in the Bronx called the Wildman. They didn't know Jessie's real name, just that she had blonde hair and fake tits and that she gave them my address and took her cut of the money when they returned after the job. That's all they knew. We talked to the owner of the Wildman, but by that time Sugarman hadn't shown up for work in weeks, and all the information they had on her in their files was wrong. You understand? She made it up. Fake name, fake address. That left me nowhere. You know how many blondes with fake tits there are in this city?

"When Sugarman was killed, my son had the idea to take the newspaper back to the club and show her picture to the owner. He said yes, it was Jessie.

"So I sent my son to Sugarman's apartment, and he found this." He took a strip of paper from his pocket, held it up for me to see. It was a torn money band, the sort banks wrap around stacks of bills. "It was behind the dresser." He put it away.

"Now it's your turn, Mr. Blake. I understand you've been going around, asking questions. I want to know everything you've learned. You see," he said, "if you find the killer, I'll find my money."

What was it I saw in his eyes? They weren't dead like his son's, they were alive, but what was it that animated them—greed? Anger? A hunger to get back what was his? He sat leaning forward, eager to hear what I had to tell him. What I felt like telling him was that he disgusted me, that sitting in the same car with him and his son made me feel physically ill. But it wasn't worth it. There were many disgusting men in the world, some of them worse than these two. If I wanted the man who killed Miranda, I had to save my energy for that fight.

"I might be able to help you," I said. "I don't know who killed her, but I'll tell you what I do know."

So I told it again, from the beginning, from waking up to Miranda's face in the paper through my second run-in with Roy. I left out the trip to Zen's—they didn't need to know about that if they didn't already. But there was no point in leaving Susan out of it, since either Roy had already told Lenz about the encounter we'd had or he would soon enough, and I assumed Lenz would tell Murco. All I left out was where she was staying now, and they seemed to accept it when I said I didn't know, that we'd separated on the subway.

"Who do you think did it?" Murco said.

"I'm going to have to think about that. Until now, you were at the top of my list."

"Was Sugarman living with anyone?" he said. "A boyfriend? A girlfriend?"

"I don't know."

"What about this old girlfriend, Mastaduno? What happened to her?"

"I don't know that either," I said. "Just that somewhere along the line she and Miranda went their separate ways."

"You think they stayed in touch?"

"I have no idea."

"It sounds to me like you've got a lot of work to do," he said. "And you understand, it's work I'd like to see done." He tapped me in the chest with the gun. "Quickly."

When it was over, I found myself back on the sidewalk across from my building, watching the sedan pull away.

For the second time this evening, I thought about taking a shower, changing my clothes—I could smell my own sweat. But I wanted to hear Leo's voice first, know that he was okay. I called the office as I climbed the stairs to my apartment. Our answering machine picked up, so I tried dialing him at home.

"This is Leo Hauser. Leave your name at the beep—"

I hung up. Maybe he was in transit. That was the good possibility. The alternative was that Roy had been waiting for him at the hotel, had overpowered him and taken his gun away, had given him the sort of beating you couldn't expect a man Leo's age to survive, no matter how tough he was. I tried the office again, hung up when I heard my own voice.

I just had to wait. I unlocked the door to my apartment. I'd try him again at home in a half hour, and if that didn't work—

One of my windows was open.

I tried to pull the door shut again, but from the side a long arm snaked around my waist and pulled me off balance. I fell to the floor and tried to roll out of the way but didn't get far before I felt one hand grab my belt and another grab a handful of my jacket collar. Then I was off the ground and in the air. I landed on the floor on the far side of my bed, the phone charger in my pocket digging into my side. The man who'd thrown me was taking the long way around the bed. The lights were off and the door had swung shut, and in the darkness I couldn't make out his face, but there were only two people I knew with a silhouette that massive, and one of them had just driven away with his father.

"Roy, stop." I looked around for something I could use as a weapon. I grabbed my desk lamp and yanked the cord out of the wall, brandished it like a club. He batted it out of my hands.

"Don't do this," I said. He grabbed the front of my jacket and pulled me close. I could smell his breath.

"Why not, motherfucker?"

Why not.

"Murco just hired me," I said.

"What?"

"Your boss. He was here, just a minute ago. With his son. They want me to do some work for them. Call them. You'll see." I couldn't stop talking. As long as I was talking, he wasn't hitting me. "His cell phone number's in my pocket. Call him. He'll be very angry if you hurt me."

I could almost see the gears turning in his head, the enormous effort it took for him to hold himself back. But Murco's name scared him.

"If you're lying . . ." he said. He didn't finish the thought. He didn't have to.

He released me with one hand and took the slip of paper from me when I dug it out of my pocket. He pulled me over to the window so he had enough light to read it. "Dial," he said and read the number off to me. I pressed the buttons on my desk phone, held the receiver out to him.

I heard someone pick up and Roy took the phone. He

was still holding tight to the front of my jacket with one huge fist.

"Mr. Khachadurian? This is Roy from the club. Yes. I'm with John Blake, he says you— Yes, in his apartment. Wayne did. Because he's sticking his nose— He's hanging around the club, he's bothering the girls— No, I haven't. Yes. Yes. Yes, I understand." He slammed the phone down.

He pulled me close again. "You're one lucky son of a bitch," he said. He shoved me back and my knees buckled against the bed. I went sprawling. Then he was standing above me, blocking what little light came in through the window. I didn't see his fist come down, but I felt it as he buried it deep in my belly.

"Murco," I croaked.

"I don't work for Murco," he hissed. "I work for Wayne Lenz." An uppercut slammed against the underside of my chin, snapping my head back against the mattress. "That's first of all. Second, I don't like getting sprayed in the eyes." One more punch, this one aimed at my groin. I turned and caught it on my hip.

"He'll kill . . . he'll kill you." I could barely get the words out.

"Well, now, that's third," he said, and I could hear the satisfaction in his voice. "The man said don't do any permanent damage. Didn't say don't hit you." The next blow caught me on the side of the head. After that, I didn't feel the rest, just heard them as they landed.

Eventually he got tired of the game. "Lucky son of a bitch," he said again.

He walked out, slammed the door behind him.

Chapter 15

The window was still open, letting the cold air in. I rolled to the edge of the bed, got my feet under me, limped over to the window, and pulled it shut. Though I knew it wouldn't do much good. This apartment was too insecure and getting a little too well known.

Moving slowly, I stuffed a duffel bag with an armful of clothes, slung it over my shoulder, grabbed the Serner files and my notebook, and made my way down to the street. There were no cabs, so I started walking. The streets were dark and empty, and the few people I saw left me alone. Bit by bit I made my way to Ninth Street.

The heated lobby was a balm at first, warming my stiff fingers and cold face, but by the time I got to the four-teenth floor the protective numbness the cold had provided had worn off and I felt sore in every part of my body. I don't have a lot of padding and, like most people, have never learned the right way to take a beating. Some of the worst of it had been absorbed by the mattress, thank God, but the rest of it had been absorbed by me, and I could still feel every spot his fists had landed. I leaned against the wall and put all my effort into pressing the doorbell. I felt like an old man.

My mother let me in. I must have looked pretty bad, because her hand flew to her mouth when she opened the door. Behind her on the living room couch, I saw Leo. Of course he'd come here, I realized belatedly—he'd had to drop off Susan's things.

"Sorry, Leo," I said. "I lost your gun."

"What happened?"

I tried to shrug, but it hurt too much. "Too much," I said. "I'll tell you in the morning. You get her stuff?"

He pointed to two suitcases next to the couch. "No problem. I didn't see anyone watching the room."

"No, you wouldn't have. They were all at my place."

I heard a toilet flush and a moment later Susan came in. Her hand flew to her mouth, too. "My God, John, what happened?"

"I'm okay," I said, but she stood there wanting more. "Just had a nice little meeting with the Murcos, pere and fils—"

"They did this to you?" she said.

"No, they were perfect gentlemen. Though they were the ones who took your gun, Leo."

"That's all right," he said, but I could see he was seething.

"Then," I said, "after they left, I had a nice little visit from Roy. Been nicer if I'd still had the gun. But I'm here."

Leo cleared a place for me on the couch and I lay down.

"Anything else you want to tell us?" Leo said.

"No," I said. "Yes. He didn't do it. Murco. He didn't kill Miranda. Someone set it up to look like he did, and he would have, but he didn't."

"Johnny, you're not making sense."

"Tomorrow," I said. I'd never realized my mother's couch was this comfortable. My eyes were closing. Someone kissed my forehead. Probably wasn't Leo.

Under the spinning lights, Miranda was dancing. Her face was the face from the newspaper, from the yearbook, and she was dressed in her graduation gown and mortarboard cap, but she was on a stage between two brass poles, and as I watched she threw the cap to the crowd and started unzipping the front of the gown. The stools on either side of me were packed and behind me men were cheering, clapping rhythmically to the beat of the music. Across the stage from me one man made a bullhorn of his hands and started shouting, *Take it off! Take it off!* until the chant spread, and now the room was echoing with the words and the sound of pounding palms. The zipper went down, down, and the V-shaped split in the gown spread, showing nothing under it but skin. Her breasts spilled out, enormous and surgically sculpted, and the men roared their approval. She shrugged the gown off and danced up to me, dropped to her knees in front of me, lifted her breasts to me with one arm and cupped the back of my head with the other. She was pressing my head forward, and behind me someone clapped me on the back and urged me on. Then her breasts were in my face, soft under my cheeks, and her skin smelled like I remembered. With her arm around my head, the sound was blocked—I could still hear it, but only from very far away. And from much closer I heard her voice, her soft voice saying, "Don't let me go, John, please, don't let me go . . ."

When I woke up, my shoes and socks were off and there was a blanket over me. My mother's bedroom door was closed and so was mine. Leo was gone, maybe back to Jersey, maybe just to the office. I wasn't the only one who occasionally spent the night on a couch, though I seemed to be doing an unusual amount of it lately.

Standing up wasn't as bad as I feared, though I'd never heard my legs or back crack so loudly. I dragged my duffel bag into the bathroom, stripped off the rest of my

clothes, and climbed into the tub. It was still dark outside
the window, but as I lay there with the hot water pouring
in and the drain open to let it out again, it slowly turned
light. My left wrist hurt—I must have twisted it when I
landed. My neck was bad, and so was my abdomen. But
the water helped, as did lying in one spot and not
moving. I flipped the lever to stop the drain and eventually turned the water off with one foot, then just lay and
soaked.

I thought about what Murco had said. Was it possible
that Miranda had dreamed up a million-dollar theft, had
talked two poor sons of bitches into pulling it off for her,
and had vanished with half the money while they were
left twisting in the wind? I thought about the girl I'd
known, the one who'd grown up with dreams of helping
people, and I told myself yes, it was possible. Because
anything's possible. Turn on the nightly news and you'll
see that every killer was a nice young man to his neighbors, a good son to his parents, a faithful parishioner at
his church. Every corporate swindler led off in cuffs had
a history of donations to the Metropolitan Museum or
the Juvenile Diabetes Foundation. Maybe my Miranda
couldn't have done the things Murco described, but my
Miranda had vanished the day she got on the plane to
New Mexico.

But *how*? There were only so many people who'd have
known that Murco was about to make a big buy. The son
would have known, presumably, but I didn't see any signs
of disloyalty there. Maybe Lenz, although the way Murco
had talked about him, it didn't sound like he was part of
the inner circle: *You think I would have left the body
there for Lenz to find? You think I'm stupid?* Certainly
the sellers—whoever Murco was giving the money to—
would have known about the buy. But that was about it.

And how would Miranda have known any of these people? She would have known Lenz, of course, from working at the Sin Factory; but would she have known any of them well enough to be in a position to hear them talking about Murco's upcoming buy and all the cash he'd have on hand the night before?

Of course, Miranda wouldn't necessarily have had to get that close to them—all she'd needed was to get that close to someone who knew them, or someone who knew someone who did. Maybe one of the gentlemen from Colombia had a girlfriend who worked at the club, and that girlfriend had shared some juicy gossip with Miranda about the big deal going down between her boy and Big Murco. Or maybe one of the girls Murco was using to pass the stuff on to the street-level dealers had been told she'd have some work to do soon, and she'd bragged about it to Miranda.

One way or another, though, Miranda had heard about the buy—and then, if Murco was to be believed, she'd gone to work. Either she'd raced up to the Bronx and gotten a job there in a hurry or more likely she'd gotten that job earlier, maybe had spent weeks or months cultivating some punch-drunk regulars she could talk into pulling a heist for her when the time came. When it did, she gave them Murco's name and address, waved goodbye from the doorstep, and waited for them to return with the loot. And why had they? There is such a thing as honor among thieves—if there weren't, no thieves would ever work together twice. But as much as I didn't like to think about it, there was probably more to it in this case: given that she'd picked these guys up at a strip club, there was probably an element of sex involved that kept them coming back to her.

It had been a bad deal for the men. If Murco was

right, once the job was finished she'd taken the money and run—although maybe 'run' wasn't quite the right word, since she'd actually stayed right here in New York, God only knew why. Meanwhile, within a few weeks her two companions had been picked up, hustled back to Scarsdale, and subjected to the third degree. Or the fourth degree. Whichever degree involved losing your teeth one by one and then getting dumped in a river or a shallow grave.

In the end, they'd given her up—as much as they'd had to give, they'd given. Begging and pleading for their lives, or maybe by the end begging and pleading to be put out of their misery, they'd told Murco everything they knew. Which wasn't much.

That left him where? He'd gotten back half the money he'd lost, and he'd gotten the people directly responsible for robbing him and beating him up—that was good. But it left the other half of the money unaccounted for, and five hundred thousand dollars wasn't peanuts to a mid-level operator like Khachadurian. More important, it left the person behind the scheme at large, having gotten away with her crime. This Murco couldn't tolerate. So he went hunting for her, and shortly thereafter she turned up dead on the roof of his club. But not by his hand, if you believed him.

Who, then? Well, who would have had a reason to kill her? One possibility: Someone who knew she had the money and wanted it for himself. Another: Someone who was afraid of her and what she might do to him. Which could be the same person—whoever had tipped her off about the upcoming buy might know, or at least suspect, that she now had the money; and that person would have plenty of reason to be afraid of her, knowing that if Murco succeeded in tracking Miranda down, she'd eventually break under Catch's tender ministrations and name her source of information. Alive, Miranda was a threat. Dead, she was worth five hundred thousand dollars.

But who was this person? Catch? Lenz? One of the gentlemen from Colombia? Either that, or someone who knew one of them intimately enough to have heard him mumbling something about the buy in his sleep. Or was I forgetting something?

There was a knock on the bathroom door. "John, are you in there?" It was Susan's voice.

I raised myself to a sitting position. "Yes. I'll be out in a minute."

"That's all right, I just wanted to know if you're okay."

I stepped out of the tub gingerly, holding onto the towel bar for balance. "Okay might be putting it too strongly," I said. "But at least I'm clean."

"That's an improvement."

I smiled. "Hang on." I wrapped a towel around my waist and opened the door. She was wearing a pair of men's flannel pajamas and holding a toothbrush and a tube of Colgate in one hand. Her hair was up, her makeup was off, and she looked—

She looked irresistible. I wanted to take her in my arms and hold her. I didn't do it, but I wanted to.

She looked me over, lingering at the old bruise over my right hip and the new ones beginning to discolor my shoulder and my left side under my arm. "Damaged goods," I said, but it didn't make her smile. "It's okay. I've had worse."

"God, John. Why do you do this?"

"Get beaten up? I try not to."

"Why do you work in a job where you have to try?"

I could have given a glib response—I'd given them often enough when other people had asked the same question. But somehow it didn't feel right this time. She was asking seriously and I owed her a serious answer. "I like to think I can do some good," I said. "Not a lot, maybe—but some. The papers, the news channels— Miranda's only been dead a few days and they're already onto the next story. The police, it's the same thing. But meanwhile, a woman was murdered. She deserved better, Susan. Even if she did the things they're saying, she didn't deserve to die for it.

"The way I look at it is, if I don't do something about it, who's going to? Now, maybe Leo's right and I'm not going to accomplish anything, but maybe he's wrong and I will. And if it takes me getting a few bruises to do it, well, I'm still better off than she is." Susan didn't say anything. "That's all."

She stepped into the bathroom, pulled the door closed behind her. She put one hand on either side of my face gently and stroked the hair above my ears. It hurt when I took her in my arms. I didn't let go.

Chapter 16

There was barely room in the bed for the two of us to lie side by side. She lay with her head on an unbruised portion of my chest and we breathed slowly, recovering. I stroked my fingertips along the back of her neck and she traced hers through the hair below my navel. Neither of us said anything.

I was thinking about how much had changed, and how little. Here I was again, in the same apartment, in the same bed, looking up at the same bookshelf. The hook was still there. Only the bird was gone.

I kissed her when she came back from her shower, then limped out to the bathroom to take one of my own. My duffel bag was still there, and I dressed in a fresh pair of jeans and a warm shirt. I was still sore, but it wasn't so bad now that some of the soreness had been gained in a good cause.

She met me at the door to my room with a handful of notes. "Let me fill you in on what I found out last night. I made a lot of calls."

"Coffee first."

I found the filters hidden in the butter compartment of the refrigerator, next to a small bag of hazelnut coffee. It was the sort of thing I'd never buy for myself, but now, as it brewed, it made me very happy. The smell was wonderful: warm and rich and domestic.

I poured each of us a cup, and Susan flattened out the first sheet of paper. "Steven Dubois. Runs a club outside Dallas called Cooter's."

"Cooter's."

"It's not as bad as it sounds. I danced there once. It's a good place for beginners, and Steven's not a bad guy. He won't push you to do anything you don't want to do. Holds open auditions and amateur nights and wet T-shirt competitions, and the crowd he gets isn't too raunchy, more southern gentlemen than good old boys."

"Southern gentlemen and wet T-shirt competitions don't sound like a natural combination."

"You'd be surprised. Anyway, I called him, and he said yes, sure, he remembered two Rianon girls showing up at his door in '96." She read from her notes. "He said they were 'green as grass, but gorgeous and game.' "

"Did he actually say that? Green and gorgeous and game?"

"That's how he talks," she said. "The first night I was there, I remember when he announced me he said 'Ladies and gentlemen, may I present, from the sunny shores of Fremont, California, the feisty and fabulous Rachel Firestone.' "

"Ladies and gentlemen?" I said.

"They get a few ladies."

"Well, I can't argue with fabulous." I drank some coffee. "Fabulous Firestone. I like it."

"You don't think I'm feisty?"

"You could teach courses in feisty. What else did Mr. Dubois have to say?"

"That's it. He remembered them, said they danced there for a couple of weeks and moved on. He said the men loved them. They did this act where they'd dance together and instead of undressing themselves, they'd undress each other."

I remembered the photo, Miranda resting her head on Jocelyn's shoulder, arm around her waist. It wasn't so hard to picture them dancing together, peeling off each other's clothes.

"The second place I found where someone remembered them was a club called Sans Souci in New Orleans." She looked up from her notes. "I'm just telling you about the yesses. There were something like twenty who said no or just weren't willing to talk to me. Your mom is going to have one hell of a long distance bill."

"That's okay."

"So, Sans Souci. I've never been there, but Matt Callan—he's a booking agent I used to work with—Matt said they hire a lot of unagented girls there. I figured Miranda and Jocelyn probably hadn't signed with an agent at this point, although I suppose they could have. Anyway, I talked to the manager, and after I got through to him that I wasn't looking for a job myself, I managed to get him to think back, and he remembered them, too. That act of theirs seems to have stuck in people's minds."

"Was it that unusual?"

"Two girls stripping each other? I haven't seen anything like it. There are girl-girl acts in the champagne rooms sometimes, but that's usually just a sex show, not a dance routine. From what people are saying, Miranda and Jocelyn had a really nice number worked out, with choreography and everything."

"Must have been something to see."

"Well, that brings us to number three. Matt told me about a guy named Morris Levy who operates a string of clubs in the Southeast. As far east as Jacksonville, as far north as Atlanta. According to Matt, he bought up a bunch of failing clubs in the eighties, renamed them Mo's, put the waitresses in hotpants and matching T-shirts, repainted the bathrooms, and reopened. The clubs are still in business twenty years later, so I guess it worked."

"You ever work at one of them?"

Susan shook her head. "Wait till you hear why. Matt said he never books his dancers at Mo's because Mo Levy has a habit of shooting videotapes of his dancers without their permission. Not just their acts—I'm talking about in the dressing room, the bathroom, the whole nine yards. All the decent agents avoid him, which means he has to rely on lots of amateurs and girls who don't know any better. A couple of dropout college girls would be a perfect fit for him."

"What does he do with these videotapes?"

"He used to sell them through classified ads in sex

papers until he got in trouble for it. These days, I don't
know, he probably swaps them over the Internet. Or
maybe he just watches them himself, or shows them to
his friends. But Matt says he never stopped making
them."

"How does he know that?"

"I told you, they all talk to each other in this business.
Word gets around."

"Okay. So you called Levy?"

She nodded. "Matt gave me his number. I asked him
about Miranda and Jocelyn, described the act, and he
knew exactly who I meant. Said they'd worked for him
for almost a year starting in 1999, going from one of his
clubs to another. They'd been a popular act, brought in a
lot of business. So I asked if he had a tape of them."

"You just asked?"

"I told him about the murder first. I explained I was
working with your firm on the investigation. He sounded
honestly upset about the whole thing. Maybe he was just
frightened, I don't know. I told him it was important that
he share with us anything he knew, and when he was
done telling me what he remembered, I asked him
whether he had any pictures or videos that would show
either of the women. He said no."

"So he didn't have anything."

"Hold on," she said. "I told him that we knew about
his history with the videotapes, we had evidence that
he'd continued to make them, and now he had two
choices: show us anything he had with Miranda and
Jocelyn on it, or wake up tomorrow morning to the cops
knocking on his door."

"Jesus."

"I also said we'd contact every dancer who'd worked in
one of his clubs and by next week he'd be buried in law-

suits. While if he sent us what he had, we'd leave him alone."

"Jesus Christ. Leo would love you. What did he say?"

She sipped her coffee. "He said I was a ball-buster. That was the nicest thing he called me, actually. It went on for a while. But in the end there wasn't much he could do. He swore he didn't have anything of the bathroom or dressing room variety, but he finally admitted he had a tape of their performance itself. You should be getting a package at your office tomorrow by express mail."

"He's sending the tape?"

"A copy of it," she said. "I don't know if it will help in any way, but I figured it couldn't hurt."

It couldn't hurt? The case, maybe. I tried to imagine what it would be like to watch Miranda perform this popular act of hers, this tandem striptease that had all the strip club patrons from New Mexico to Florida talking. Susan reached across the table to put a hand on my arm.

"You don't have to watch it," she said. "I can watch it for you, tell you if there's anything on it you need to know about."

I shook my head. "No. It's just a different type of bruising I've got to take. Leo warned me when this all started that I wouldn't like what I learned. Doesn't change what I've got to do, though."

She took her hand back, folded the papers. "I've got some more calls out from yesterday and another twenty or so places to call today. We've still got three years to fill in and they're nowhere near New York."

"And they're still dancing together."

"Right. So there's plenty of work left. I'll do what I can."

"Thank you," I said. "I really appreciate it, Susan."

"I like it, actually. It's interesting work, and it keeps my mind occupied. Keeps me from thinking too much about how I'm going to get by with no job, and probably no one willing to hire me."

"You could always go to work as a detective," I said. "You seem to have a knack for it."

"What about you? What are you going to do?"

"Murco told me she recruited the burglars at a club in the Bronx. I figured I'd pay it a visit."

"Be careful," Susan said.

I squeezed her hand.

"If you need anything, you can give me a call," she said. "If I'm on the phone here, you can try me on my cell. I programmed the number into your phone while you were in the shower."

"You think that's safe? Trusting me with your number?"

"I decided to take the chance," she said.

Chapter 17

The Wildman was about as different from the Sin Factory as two places could get. The building was only one story tall but it sprawled over what in Manhattan would have been the footprint of a skyscraper. The parking lot out back could have fit four brownstones. The walls looked like they'd been made from stacked cinderblocks and the roof was just slanted enough to let the snow slide off in the winter. There was a lighted bill-board out front, but no doorman or bouncer, and even standing right under the front awning you couldn't hear a thing from inside.

Down the block and across the avenue were car lots and a mini-mall featuring a food court, a karate studio, and a combination Carvel ice cream store and video rental place. None of these establishments seemed to be doing much business.

Neither was the Wildman, but that wasn't a surprise given that it wasn't even noon yet. Only hardcore alcoholics crack their first pint in the morning, and the same was true of strip club devotees. At noon or one you might see some local businessmen taking in the sights over lunch, but in the morning the clientele was limited to the addicted, the unemployed, and a few bleary-eyed night shift workers just getting off the job.

But "24-Hour Action!" was one of the things the Wildman advertised on its sign, so it had to be open for business. I pushed through the door, paid the twenty-dollar cover to the man behind the barred bank teller window, and stepped through the curtain of heavy plastic strips that separated the front room from the back.

My eyes took a moment to adjust. This room took up most of the rest of the building's space, with five platform stages and a long wooden walkway snaking from one to the next. At the far end there was a full-sized stage with a red curtain and no one in front of it. Two of the five platforms were occupied, one by a tall woman with a Grace Jones flattop and small, natural breasts, the other by a woman closer to my height, chunkier, wearing silver hoops through her nipples and an ankh tattoo at the base of her throat. Her breasts looked natural, too. I hadn't realized you could still find strippers with natural breasts in New York, even if you went to the Bronx at eleven in the morning.

A few of the stools were occupied, though most were

still stacked upside down on their tables. In one corner of
the room a bartender was setting up, ripping open boxes
of beer bottles and packing them into a cooler. There was
a wooden bowl full of nuts and pretzels, and I grabbed a
handful, popped them one by one while I waited for the
bartender to come over.

"Not open yet, champ," he said. "Another half hour."

"Danny Matin around?"

"This early? You're joking, man."

"So who's here?"

"You and me, man." He finished the box of Budweiser,
started in on a box of Coors. "What you want Danny for
anyway?"

I flashed my wallet open and shut, giving him a
glimpse of something that might have been a badge.
"Girl who used to dance here was involved in a robbery,
later turned up dead downtown. We're investigating the
connection."

"You talking about Jessie? That girl was bad news.
Everybody knew it."

"What do you mean?"

He came over, rested his forearms on the bar. "She
was always asking for trouble. Guys you wouldn't want to
run into on the street, she'd take them in the V.I.P. room
two at a time. Nice little white girl like her and she takes
these guys twice her size in the back. More prison tats
they got, more she likes them."

"And what would she do back there?"

"I don't know, man, but whatever it was it must have
been good, since most of the time they came back for
more. Wasn't the type of repeat business Danny really
wanted. He was glad, I'll tell you, when she stopped
showing up. Although we was worried maybe she'd got
herself hurt or killed. Which I guess she did."

It fit. If she was trying to recruit a pair of strongarm types to carry out a job, this was the sort of place to do it. It sounded like she'd had her pick of the Bronx's tough male population.

"What shift did she work?"

"It varied. Some weeks, she'd be working now, ten to three. Some weeks she'd do the graveyard shift, two a.m. to seven. Never saw her work prime time. She wasn't a prime time kind of girl."

That fit, too: she couldn't be in two places at once, and the hours he was calling prime time were probably the ones she spent at the Sin Factory.

I took out a photocopy of the picture that had run in the *Daily News*, unfolded it, and handed it to him. "Just for the record, is this her?"

He only looked at it for a second. "Yeah. I mean, she looked different when she was dancing here, but yeah, could be her."

"Could be?"

"Man, you show me a xerox of a photo from a news-paper from when she was in, what's that, high school? College? Best I can say is could be. You show me a black girl, I'd say couldn't be."

"So all you're really saying is that this girl and the one you knew as Jessie were both white?"

"No, man. That girl looks right. I don't know." He looked at the picture again, handed it back. "It's just that she'd grown up a lot since that picture was taken."

We all have, I said. But I said it to myself.

I left a card with him to give to Danny Matin when Matin got in. Matin was the owner; I didn't expect him to be able to tell me anything more than he'd told Catch, assuming he ever called, but you never find out if you don't ask. I hadn't gotten much out of the bartender, but I didn't consider it a wasted trip. I'd wanted to see the place Miranda had danced, the place where she'd picked up the men who'd robbed Murco. When you put together a puzzle, not every piece is equally important— some just show a bit of the sky, not George Washington's head. But you don't have a complete picture until every piece is in place.

I rode the subway back to Manhattan. It gave me plenty of time to think. When I'd called Murco to get Matin's name, I'd also asked him for Miranda's address, and that's where I was headed now. What would I find there? Probably nothing, because that's pretty much what Catch had found when he'd searched the place. But again, I wanted the whole picture, and for that I needed to see the place where she'd lived, the place where Murco's money had gone missing.

"You're wasting your time," Murco had said. "We've already been over the place. There's nothing to see."

"With all due respect, you're not a detective, and neither is your son."

"The police have been over it, too."

"You're going to tell me the police never miss anything?"

This got a laugh out of him, or something like a laugh. It was a nasty sound. "You can look if you want, Mr. Blake. But the clock's ticking, and I'm not a patient man."

"Neither am I," I said.

I wondered what he would do if I did find something and what I found suggested that the person who had tipped Miranda off about the buy was someone close to him. A betrayal by one of the men he bought drugs from might not come as a surprise, but what if it was his own son or the club manager he'd worked with for years?

"How sure are you that Miranda got half the money?"

"Very."

"They couldn't have been lying to you, trying to hold something back?"

"Oh, they tried. That didn't last long."

"Well, if she had the money in her apartment at one point and it's not there now, that means someone took it. I don't think it was the police—they'd be working harder on this case than they are if they'd found half a million dollars in cash in a murder victim's apartment. That means the money was probably taken out of the apartment by whoever killed her. And if that's the case, someone in the building might have seen something, or heard something—"

"You're just fishing."

"Of course I'm fishing—what do you think detective work is?"

"All I have to say, Mr. Blake, is that you'd better catch something. Soon."

Before heading up to the Bronx, I'd also called Leo and brought him up to speed on where things stood. I figured maybe he'd be able to see some connection I'd missed or suggest a path I hadn't thought of pursuing. But all he'd said was the same thing Susan had, which was that I should be careful.

"You've already managed to get two dangerous men angry at you. Wayne and Roy. You seem to be in good for the time being with the Khachadurians, but who knows how long that will last. Then there's this girl you've planted in your mother's apartment—she seems okay, but the truth is you don't know whether you can count on her."

"I'm not worried about that," I said. "But Murco's another story. On one hand, what's he going to do to me if I don't turn up the killer? On the other hand, what if I do and it turns out to be someone close to him, which it pretty much has to be?"

"Like we used to say in the army, one way you're screwed, the other you're fucked. That's why I'm telling you to be careful."

"Don't you have any other advice?" I'd asked. "You always have advice."

"I gave you my advice five days ago. I told you to stay out of it. You didn't listen. Now you're just going to have to see it through to the end."

The train squealed to a stop, and a voice over the loud-speaker said, "Eighth Avenue, last stop. Transfer for the A, C, and E lines . . ."

I pushed out of the car, joined the midday crowd elbowing its way up to the street. I kept one hand firmly on the flap of my jacket pocket as I climbed the crowded stairs.

"Can I at least come by," I'd asked Leo, "and pick up the other gun?"

"Yeah," he'd said, "maybe you'd better."

Chapter 18

I checked the address against the slip of paper I'd written it down on. It was a converted loft building on the far West Side, one of the neighborhoods in Manhattan that still looks the way it did fifty years ago. On the outside, at least—inside, the building had new elevators, a lobby sporting wire sculptures and recessed track lights, and no doubt rents that weren't easy to pay even if your income was tax-free. I watched through the glass panel of the door as a man in a heavy overcoat came out of the elevator. I stepped out of his way as he left the building, and he held the door for me. I thanked him and went inside.

The slip of paper said 4-J, so I rode the elevator to the fourth floor and followed the corridor past the gerrymandered chunks of what had once been warehouse space. Landlords in New York know a thing or two about making silk purses: throw up a few sheetrock walls and your derelict industrial building can rent for thousands to hungry young things who can't afford to live in midtown but don't want the indignity of moving to Brooklyn or Queens. 4-J was the last apartment on the floor, and having been in a few loft buildings before, I knew it was probably the smallest, made up of whatever space had been left over after the rest of the floor was laid out. I had no key, but Catch Khachadurian hadn't had one either. I slid an expired MasterCard between the door and the jamb and drove it up sharply against the tongue of the latch. If the deadbolt had been on, it wouldn't have done me any good, but why would anyone have locked the deadbolt on a dead woman's apartment? In any event, no one had. The door popped open.

The place was small all right, though I'd seen smaller. One wall had a bank of old-fashioned mullioned windows set into naked brick and a rack radiator clanking out heat. A frameless futon lay against the neighboring wall, a few copies of *Cosmo* and *Us* piled neatly at the foot. The floor was bare but clean. The walls were empty. Either the apartment's previous visitors had stripped the place or Miranda had lived a pretty spartan life in it. She probably hadn't spent a lot of time at home, I figured. There certainly wasn't much temptation to, and as I looked around I could appreciate the appeal a windfall of five hundred

thousand dollars must have held for her. It wasn't mil-
lions, it wasn't an amount to kill or get killed over, you'd
never make a movie about people trying to steal that
little, but if you had it, you could get yourself a real bed, a
real apartment in a better part of town, a rug for the floor,
maybe some pictures for the walls, instead of spending
every dollar you earned just to keep the landlord at bay.

The far side of the room doubled as the kitchen, a
small counter separating the two-burner electric stove on
one side from the sink on the other. There was a minia-
ture refrigerator under the sink, a pair of cabinets over it.
The refrigerator had a couple of apples that had started
to go soft, a sugar bowl she presumably kept there to
keep the bugs out of it, two cans of tuna, half a lemon.
The cabinet contained a half-finished box of Lipton tea
bags, a few dishes, two mugs.

There was no closet. What there was instead was a tall
chest of drawers, and inside I found piles of clothing. Not
neatly folded, but that was to be expected given that
they'd been rifled through at least twice. Lots of T-shirts,
a few sweaters, some skirts and dresses. Underwear. It
felt strange going through her clothes. This was the
closest I'd come to Miranda in ten years, and the closest I
ever would. I could smell her on her clothing, the quiet,
simple, lived-in smell any dresser full of clothing gets
over time, and if it wasn't quite the smell I remembered,
it was close enough to trigger all sorts of memories.

The bras I found gave me a sense of the size she'd
chosen to make her breasts, and it was definitely an
increase, though not of the Mandy Mountains variety. I
kept waiting to find her costumes, her work clothes, and
in the bottom drawer I finally did. Thin gowns, a Lycra
bodysuit, g-strings in various colors, front-clasp satin

bras, elbow-length gloves. A few pairs of shoes. A tangle of stockings.

A narrow hallway led to a surprisingly large bathroom. The medicine cabinet was open a few inches, and when I tried to close it the door swung open again. Not much inside—a few tubes of lipstick, some eyebrow pencils, eye shadow. A nasal inhaler for congestion. A small bottle of Anbesol and a large bottle of nail polish remover, a plastic bag of three hundred cotton balls that now held something more like fifty, a small tube of toothpaste squeezed almost to the end. No toothbrush, or hairbrush either, but I figured the police had probably taken those. It was the easiest way to get material for the sort of DNA test Kirsch had told me the police had run. What surprised me more was that I didn't see any of the things you'd expect from a contact lens wearer—no saline, no lens case, no spares. Maybe the police took those things, too, or maybe I was wrong and she hadn't switched to contacts. Maybe she'd had laser surgery done by one of the crack ophthalmologists at Rianon, or else one of the dozen who advertised on the subway here in the city.

I returned to the living room. What else was there to see? There were no other rooms. I lifted the futon, pulled the dresser away from the wall. There were no more torn paper bands. The phone on top of the dresser still had a dial tone and the twelve-inch television sitting on the floor still had reception, so neither the telephone company nor the cable company had switched off her service yet. Maybe no one had notified them.

I flipped through the pages of the magazines, but nothing fell out other than a few blow-in subscription cards. I put them back. Hanging from a hook on the front door was a maroon cloth baseball cap and a light blue denim jacket. Searching the pockets only produced a crumpled tissue and a foil-wrapped roll of breath mints.

The apartment was as bare as a hotel room. Some clothes, some bits of food, a portable TV set, a phone—it was the home of someone accustomed to picking up and leaving on a moment's notice, someone used to carrying everything she owned in the trunk of a car. For how many years had Miranda been on the road? Five? Six? For all I knew, she might only have come back to New York right before getting the job at the Sin Factory. If she'd lived longer, maybe she'd eventually have put down roots, but it hadn't happened yet.

Of course, she'd already had roots in the city once. Her mother. Me. I couldn't help wondering whether, if she'd lived longer and had stayed in the city, she would ever have called me. Or even whether she had. Like everyone else, I occasionally found empty messages on my answering machine, was the victim of late night hang-up calls. Could one of them have been her?

Or had she tried to look me up and been stymied by my unlisted number? If I'd been listed, might she have reached me and let me help her?

Maybe. Maybe. It didn't make any difference now.

I looked out through the peephole to make sure the hallway was empty before letting myself out.

There was no 4-I, and knocking on the door to 4-H produced no result. But 4-G was home: I could hear the radio going through the door and heard its volume drop after I knocked. Footsteps shuffled toward me and I heard the plastic peephole cover slide up.

"Yes?"

"Sorry to bother you," I said. "My name is John Blake, and I'm investigating the death of one of your neighbors,

Miranda Sugarman." I held my investigator's license up in front of the peephole.

"I don't know anyone named Sugarman."

"She lived in 4-J, just down the hall."

"Oh, the girl Winston rented to. That must be why all the police were here on Sunday. I didn't realize she'd died." I heard locks turning and then the door swung in, but only a little. In the narrow space between door and wall an old woman's face appeared. "Are you with the police?"

"No," I said, "I'm a private investigator. Also a friend of the Sugarman family."

"Oh." She brought a hand up to scratch her chin. "What happened?"

"Ms. Sugarman was found dead Sunday morning at the club where she worked," I said. "I'm trying to find out about anything that might have happened in the days leading up to her death. Did you see her at all, or see anyone else coming or going from her apartment?"

"It's not her apartment, it's Winston's. But he hasn't lived there for a long time." She lowered her voice. "We're not supposed to sublet, but a lot of people in the building do it. You know, under the table. Everyone looks the other way."

"How long had she been living there?"

"Six months? Seven months?" She looked at me as though I might know which was right. "I said hello to her the day she moved in, so I should remember. Winston was with her. It was in April, so what's that, eight months?"

I nodded.

"She was very pretty. I thought maybe she was his girl-friend, but he said no, she was just someone who was taking the apartment."

"Did you ever talk to her?"

"Talk to her? I hardly ever saw her." She shook her head. "Coming and going late at night, and always in a rush. I'd hear her in the hallway, but by the time I'd look out she was already gone."

"Do you remember her having any visitors?"

"Sure, once in a while."

"Recently?"

"Let me think." I waited. "The walls are so thin, you can hear everything going on in the hallway. You hear people coming and going all the time. 4-J? I don't know. The policemen asked the same thing, and I told them I couldn't be sure."

"Do you remember seeing anyone in the hallway on New Year's Eve or the next day?"

"New Year's Eve, sure. There were people coming and going all night. Going to parties, coming home at one in the morning. Very noisy. And then the police came later on Sunday morning, of course."

"How about earlier in the day on Saturday? Did you see anyone going into her apartment or leaving?"

"I don't stand at the door all day watching who's in the hallway," she said.

"I know, I understand, I just thought you might remember if someone came by—"

"Just because I'm home all day doesn't mean I'm one of those busybodies who minds everyone else's business."

"I'm sure you don't," I said. "But if you happened to notice anything, if you saw or heard anything, it could make an enormous difference." I glanced at the label under the peephole. "Mrs. Krieger, this is a murder investigation. If you know anything, it's important that you share it with us."

"The last time I saw anyone going to that apartment," she said slowly, "was maybe a week ago. I was taking out the garbage, and when I came back from the incinerator room, I saw a young woman ringing the doorbell. I think that's the last time I saw someone going to 4-J, except for when the cable company sent someone."

"What did this woman look like?"

She shrugged with her eyebrows as well as her shoulders. "I just saw her from the back for two seconds."

"Did Miranda open the door?"

"I don't know, I imagine so." She thought about it for a moment. "Yes, I remember I heard the door close."

"And you don't remember anything about this woman?"

"No," she said. "Just that she was holding flowers."

"Flowers?"

"Wrapped up in paper, like you get in the street. I remember that." She shifted her weight from one foot to the other, grimaced as she settled into the new position. "That's all I remember."

"Did she have dark hair, blond hair—"

"Blond hair, I think. She was wearing one of those hats, like the teenagers wear, but under it I'm pretty sure her hair was blond."

A woman with blond hair wearing a hat and carrying flowers. The flowers made me think of Jocelyn, but that was silly—it could have been anyone.

The hat, on the other hand, made me think of the cap I'd found on the inside of Miranda's door. "Do you remember what color the hat was?" I asked.

She strained to remember. "Red? Dark red, almost purple."

That was the hat, all right. Whoever had worn it had

apparently left it behind. Which was all well and good, but it didn't tell me anything about what happened to Murco's money.

"Are you sure there was no one who visited her more recently than that? Maybe on the afternoon of the thirty-first or the morning of the first?" I tried to picture how large a package containing half a million dollars in hundred-dollar bills might be. Also how heavy. "Maybe someone carrying a shopping bag or a satchel, or maybe a suitcase?"

She shook her head helplessly. "Just the man from the cable company. He had one of those cases on wheels, the kind you pull with a handle. But no one with a suitcase or a bag."

"The cable company sent someone on New Year's Day?"

"No, this was Saturday, maybe five o'clock. I was surprised, too. Usually their service is terrible, and on a holiday evening, forget it. But the reception's been so bad, someone must have complained."

"And he went to 4-J?"

"I don't know, maybe it was 4-H—I just saw him coming this way on his way out. I tried to get him to come take a look at my cable, too, but he said I'd have to call for an appointment. He was quite rude."

"And he was pulling a case?"

"Sure, for his equipment."

"Mrs. Krieger," I said, "what did this man look like?"

"I don't know. He was young—not like you, but young. Maybe forty. Very short."

"When you say short . . . was he shorter than me?"

"Oh, yes. Much shorter."

Much shorter. "Did he have dark hair? Slick, dark hair?"

"Oh, yes. It looked very greasy. These workers they send over aren't very clean, you know."

Very short. Greasy hair. That could describe any of ten thousand men in New York, maybe more. But not in this case. In this case, it described one man: Wayne Lenz. "What made you think he was with the cable company?" I asked.

"Well, he told me, of course. When I came out in the hallway and asked him what he was doing. And he had those things hanging on his belt, those tools they use."

God only knew what he'd hung on his belt, and God only knew what he'd told this old busybody when she'd stuck her head out in the hall and asked him to fix her cable. But I had a feeling I knew what had been in the rolling case.

Five hundred thousand dollars.

Chapter 19

I was on the street again, and suddenly it was freezing. The wind had picked up while I was inside and I could feel it through my clothes. I pulled my jacket closer around me, felt the weight of Leo's pistol inside the pocket.

Lenz. It made sense. Here you had a two-time loser, a two-bit con man working in a strip club because he's never managed to make a real score, and along comes the score he's been waiting for: his boss is about to make a buy for a million dollars in cash. He had to go for it.

But not by himself, because physically he's not exactly

a powerhouse, and anyway what if he gets caught? He knows what Murco would do to him. So he gets one of the girls to work with him. He picks a loner who doesn't talk to the other girls much, a girl who doesn't entirely fit in. Because no matter how many years she'd been doing it, I couldn't believe Miranda would ever entirely fit in—she'd been a pre-med at Rianon, for God's sake.

And then he cooks up a plan that gives both of them an extra layer of protection: she'll recruit some toughs from another part of the city to do the dirty work, they'll get their cut, and Miranda and Lenz will split what's left. Yes, Lenz will only walk away with a few hundred thousand instead of a million this way, but by his standards that's still big money, and it beats taking the personal risk of being the guy who actually holds Murco Khachadurian at gunpoint.

But something goes wrong. The men who pulled the job get caught. They talk, and Lenz hears that they've talked—maybe Catch tells him in a moment of ill-advised gloating. And now all bets are off. If the men who did the job talked, that means Miranda's life isn't worth a damn. And if Miranda has a chance to talk, Lenz's life won't be worth a damn either.

That's if she talks. On the other hand, if what she does is die, he gets to keep the whole five hundred thousand instead of half of it, or whatever split they'd agreed to. And with Miranda dead, maybe Murco will stop looking for more culprits. Even if he doesn't, how is he going to tie Lenz to the burglary? Lenz presumably took precautions not to be seen with Miranda. To hammer home his innocence, he doesn't run away after shooting her, he stays right there by the body and phones for an ambulance. Would a guilty man do that?

It wasn't a complete picture, and the pieces I did have didn't all fit perfectly. There was the problem of the murder weapon: how had Lenz gotten rid of it before the police arrived? And there was the timing: Miranda must have taken the job at the Wildman long before Lenz could have heard about this particular buy Murco was going to make. Realistically, how far back could he have started setting this plan up? But enough of the pieces fit, and I didn't feel like waiting around for more to fall into place.

I flipped my cell phone open and stepped into a doorway to get out of the wind. I brought up the phone's directory, thumbed through the entries until I found the new one for "Susan F." I realized as the phone dialed that I still didn't know what the 'F' stood for. Probably not Firestone.

Susan picked up on the third ring. "The afternoon of the murder, Lenz came to Miranda's apartment, dressed as a cable guy," I said. "He must have picked a time when he knew Miranda wasn't there, found the money, and taken it out in his equipment trunk."

"Are you sure?"

"Someone saw him, a neighbor. The description fits."

"Does that mean he killed her?"

"Not necessarily," I said. "But it's sure starting to look that way."

"What are you going to do?"

"I'm going to go talk to him and find out. Do you know where he lives? Did he ever say anything while you were working for him?"

"I know he came to work by train. He was always complaining about the 7 train and the long ride he had," she said. "That's all I know."

"That's plenty."

"John, be careful. Wayne's an angry man and he could get violent."

"He's not the only one," I said.

I caught the 1 to Times Square and got on the 7 just as the doors were closing. An announcement came over the speakers as the train began its long, slow trek out to Flushing. I couldn't understand what it said, but I wasn't really trying.

After almost an hour, the train let out at Main Street and Roosevelt Avenue. This intersection was as cosmopolitan as Flushing got: a jumble of Asian restaurants and grocery stores, drug stores selling vials of ginseng alongside the out-of-season Coppertone displays, newsstands carrying foreign papers and international calling cards. A video store was promoting the latest Chow Yun-Fat import, a film whose two-character Chinese title was translated as *A Sound of Distant Drums*. The signs over the doors at McDonald's and Citibank were covered with Asian lettering. Scattered here and there were remnants of the old Flushing: a Macy's outlet store advertising a sale on men's suits and bedding, a bakery with a small sign in one corner of the window certifying it as kosher. The sidewalk was packed, and everyone on it was dressed more warmly than I was. I pushed through, hands in my pockets.

I'd had an hour in which to calm down and change my mind about confronting Lenz, but the trip had had the opposite effect on me.

Once I was off Roosevelt, the neighborhood quickly reverted to Queens normal: six-story red brick buildings interspersed with occasional stretches of one- and two-story homes, tiny patches of lawn squeezed in between the sidewalks and the facades. I passed Union and turned in on Bowne.

The telephone operator had found two listings for "W. Lenz" in the 718 area code, but only one was located on the 7 line. That W. Lenz lived here, in a building whose chipped cornerstone said it had been built in MCMXLI. The front door wasn't locked, and the one just past the vestibule, which normally would have been, was held open with a rubber doorstop. Someone was moving out, maybe, or bringing a package in from his car. It would just be a minute, and in the meantime why not leave the door propped open? Being able to leave your door open was why you lived in Flushing instead of Manhattan.

Lenz's name was listed on the intercom board next to a button marked 3-B. I didn't push it.

I started up the stairs. Normally, when you have a sense of déjà vu you can't explain the feeling, but it wasn't hard to understand it now. I climbed carefully, slowly, hugging the wall and placing each foot gently to make as little noise as possible. No one passed me on the stairs, but I kept the gun in my pocket just in case.

The second floor smelled of someone's late lunch or early dinner. The third floor didn't smell of anything. There were four apartments on the floor, with B facing A at one end of the hall. I took the gun out before I got to the door and listened at the door before I knocked. Nothing.

Was he not home? Had he already left for work? I knocked, and when I didn't get an answer, I knocked again, louder.

"Yeah? Who is it?"

It was his voice. I felt my blood rising. "Officer Michael Stern from Midtown South. I have some questions for you, Mr. Lenz."

"Jesus fucking Christ." I heard a chain slide back. "You people never stop." The top lock turned, then the bottom lock. The door opened a crack. "What is—"

I didn't wait for the rest of the sentence. I set the heel of one foot against the door and shoved inward hard, bringing my gun up as I stepped inside. Lenz stumbled backwards, against the arm of a recliner. The door banged against the inside wall, swung back and slammed shut. I advanced on him. I saw it in his eyes when he recognized me. "Keep your hands where they are," I said. "Don't reach for your pockets or you're a dead man. Turn around. Turn around!" I gestured for him to put his hands on the back of the chair, then spread his legs with one foot and patted him down one-handed the way Leo had taught me. I stepped back and he turned to face me again.

"What the fuck is this?" he said.

"Shut up." I risked a quick look to the left and right. The apartment was apparently a one bedroom, since there were only three doors leading out of the living room. The one in the far wall was open and led to a small kitchen. One of the others would lead to a bathroom, the other to the bedroom. There was a Pat Nagel print on one wall of a woman in the act of peeling off a leotard, one breast exposed, and a Leroy Neiman poster of two boxers going at it in multicolored fury. "Sit down and put your hands in your lap."

He looked like he was going to argue, but I took a step forward with the gun aimed at his head. He sat down. "I should've taken care of you that night in the club," he said.

"Maybe you should have. But you didn't, and now I'm here. And you're going to answer my goddamn questions or I'm going to put a hole in your head bigger than the ones you gave Miranda. That's right, Lenz. I know what you did."

"Fuck you," he said in a voice of utter contempt. "You don't know a fucking thing."

I could understand, suddenly, how Murco could have sat by while his son pulled those burglars' teeth one by one.

"I don't know anything?" I said. "Try me. I know about Miranda dancing at the Wildman. I know how you tipped her off about the buy and had her recruit the men who actually carried out the burglary. I know what Murco did to those men and I know that you were scared to death he'd do the same to you if she gave you up. I know you went to Miranda's apartment and stole five hundred thousand dollars, took it out of her apartment in a phony cable company equipment case. And I know that later that night you took Miranda up to the roof of the Sin Factory and put two bullets through the back of her head."

"You're so wrong it's not even funny," he said. "I never stole any money from her and I never killed anyone in my life. Get that?"

I shook my head. "Don't even try it, Lenz. I may not have enough hard evidence to put you in jail, but frankly that's not what I'd be worried about if I were you. I have enough to convince Murco." His face went pale. "That's right. Now we're speaking the same language. He wants to know where his money is, and all I have to do is tell him you have it and you'll wish I'd shot you instead."

His voice dropped to a hoarse whisper. "I don't have the money, I swear to God," he said. "But what if I could get my hands on it? What if I agreed to split it with you?"

"I don't want the money, you stupid son of a bitch. What I want you can't give me. I want Miranda back. I want her to be alive again, and unless you can give me that, don't try to offer me anything."

His eyes looked desperate. His head was twitching sharply from side to side, like it had in the club.

"Now, you're going to answer some simple questions," I said. "I want to know how you talked Miranda into going along with your plan, I want to know what you did with the gun after you shot her, and I want to know where the money is. You answer those questions and I'll ask some more. Maybe if you tell the truth I'll be better to you than you deserve and turn you over to the police rather than to Murco. Give me enough facts to get a conviction and maybe it'll save your life."

He was sweating fiercely and his eyes were darting around the room. I was watching them and his hands. That was my mistake.

How could the bedroom door have opened without my noticing? How could someone have come up behind me so silently? Maybe it was the combination of a light step and a carpeted floor working against me, or maybe I was just so focused on Lenz that I would have missed the footfalls of an elephant. More likely both.

I pieced this all together later. At the time, I only knew that there was someone behind me when Lenz smiled, a look of relief blossomed on his face, and something heavy smashed into the back of my head.

Chapter 20

I came out of it slowly, feeling the throbbing of my pulse behind my ear and the rough weave of the carpet under my cheek. At first, when I opened my eyes I couldn't see anything, then objects began to swim darkly into view: the base of the recliner, the legs of a table. The darkness wasn't a problem with my eyes, or at least not entirely. The sun had set while I was out and there were no lights on in the room.

My head swam when I tried to sit up, so I lay down again, closed my eyes. The back of my head felt pulpy when I touched it and my fingers came away wet. I probably had a concussion. I was lucky to have woken up at all.

I waited till the urge to vomit passed and tried very slowly to sit up again. When that worked, I took a few deep breaths and forced myself onto my knees. I let my head settle. Slowly, carefully, I stood up. I held my arms out to balance myself and swayed a little when finally upright.

To the light switch was only five steps. I covered the distance slowly, leaning against the wall all the way.

I wasn't ready for the light. The room came slowly into focus. I had a pounding headache, but the rest of me felt the same is it had before—whoever had clocked me hadn't taken the opportunity to do any further damage, and what surprised me more, neither had Lenz. This despite the fact that he'd had my gun lying right there. Speaking of which—

I spotted the gun by the foot of the recliner, next to

where I'd been lying a moment earlier. And that made even less sense. I could imagine reasons Lenz might not kill me—he knew I had some tie to Murco now, he was in deep enough already and didn't want another capital charge on his head, he was in a rush to get away—but I couldn't think of a reason he would have left my gun behind. I bent at the knees, lowered myself slowly to pick it up.

It smelled like it had been fired. But I hadn't pulled the trigger—unless when I was hit I'd pulled it by reflex. Did that sort of thing happen? I didn't know. I didn't think so. And in this particular case I knew it hadn't, since I'd been aiming at Lenz and he'd been sitting in the recliner. He wasn't there now and there was neither a hole nor a bloodstain in the back of the chair.

I looked around the room. The bedroom door was open and I staggered to it, even though I knew I'd find nothing. Surely the money was long gone along with Lenz.

And maybe it was—but he wasn't.

Wayne Lenz was lying on his side on the floor, one arm flung up beside his head, the other clamped to his belly. His shirt was soaked with blood. So was the carpet beneath him. His mouth and eyes were open and the look on his face—was I just imagining the shock, the look of betrayal?

I felt the gun weighing heavily in my hand. I could put it down, wipe it off, but what would that accomplish? It was registered to Leo. I could take it with me, drop it down a sewer grate on the way to the subway, hope no one saw me leave and that no one had seen me arrive—

The idea flickered briefly and died. For one thing, I was still unsteady and couldn't face two flights of stairs on my own, much less the walk back to Main Street. For another, what were the odds that no one would see me along the way?

I slipped the gun into my jacket pocket and dropped to a squat next to Lenz's body. He'd been shot at least twice, once in the gut and once in the chest. It would have been the chest shot that had killed him. I looked at his clenched fingers and decided that the look on his face might only be pain.

I took out my cell phone and speed-dialed Leo at the office. On a Friday night he'd normally be long gone, but given everything that was going on, I was hoping he'd decided to stick around.

"Come on," I said as it rang. "Leo, pick up."

The answering machine picked up instead and I heard my own voice asking me to leave a message. "Leo, I need your help. Call me back as soon as—"

The machine cut off with a beep. "Johnny?"

"Leo, we've got a problem."

"What is it?"

I stood up, moved away from the body. The bedroom rug was charcoal gray and leading toward the door I could see two parallel streaks, the sort that might have been made by the wheels of a piece of luggage after rolling over a patch of bloody carpet. "I'm in Flushing," I said, "at Wayne Lenz's apartment. He's—" I looked at the body. Leo had strong feelings about what you did and didn't say over a cell phone, because you never knew who was listening in with a shortwave. But fuck it. "He's dead. Shot twice, once through the heart. There was someone else in the apartment, came up behind me and knocked me out with something heavy, then used my gun to shoot him. Your gun, I mean."

"Damn it," Leo said. "Did you touch anything?"

"Just the gun."

"Just the gun?"

"Leo, I—"

"Forget it. Just give me the address." I gave it to him. "Stay there. Don't touch anything else, don't move anything. I'm going to call some people, but I'm not sure what I can do. The local precinct will want to handle it, and I don't know anyone in Queens."

"Next time I get framed for murder, I'll try to do it in Manhattan."

"This is not a joke. You're going to be arrested. I'll try to get them to listen, but Johnny, every murderer has a story. Every one of them, and plenty of times it's how they were knocked out and when they woke up, there was a dead body and they didn't know how it got there. It won't look good."

"Neither does the back of my head, Leo."

"You wouldn't be the first man to smash himself in the head to get out of a murder charge."

"Leo—you don't think I did it, do you?"

He said no, but I heard the moment of hesitation.

"I was knocked unconscious, Leo, and someone else— I don't know who—took my gun, shot Lenz with it, and walked out with a trunk full of money. You've got to believe me."

"I've got to," Leo said. "The police don't."

Leo was with them when they showed up at the door. They rang up from the lobby and I buzzed them in, just as if I lived there and they were coming for a friendly visit. *Won't you sit down? No, not there, that's evidence.*

There were three men with Leo, two middle-aged uniformed cops and one in plain clothes who looked about thirty years old except that he was balding like an old man. One of the uniforms took me by the arm and started reading me my rights while the other headed for the bedroom.

"Do you understand these rights as I've explained them to you?"

I looked at the name stitched above his breast pocket. "Yes, Officer Lyons, I understand. You're going to want this." I picked up my jacket, which I'd taken off and left by the door. "There's a gun in the pocket. I touched it—I shouldn't have, but I did, I'd been hit on the head and wasn't thinking straight. But there may still be other prints on it." He took the jacket. "Also, I've looked around for the object the person who hit me might have used, and I couldn't find it. But I did find this." I walked him over to the recliner, and next to where I'd been lying there was a piece of frosted glass. It looked like a horse's head. "It probably broke off from a bigger piece, some sort of heavy glass sculpture, maybe a cowboy on horseback, something like that. You might find it thrown out somewhere on this block or in the neighborhood."

"John," Leo said gently. "Let them do their job."

"I'm letting them, I'm just pointing a few things out."

"If there's something to find, we'll find it," Lyons said.

The plainclothes cop came forward. "I'll watch him, Lyons. You can go check out the body."

Lyons looked like he wasn't sure he wanted to let go of me, but the tone in the plainclothes man's voice suggested he wasn't just making an offer. Lyons released my arm and went to join his partner in the bedroom.

"Blake, you're in deep shit. Leo filled me in."

His voice had sounded familiar, and now I placed it. "Kirsch?"

He nodded. "I don't have jurisdiction here, but if I can tie this in with Sugarman, maybe they'll let us take it over."

"Oh, you can tie it in with Sugarman all right. That I promise you."

Leo had followed Lyons to the bedroom and now he came back. "What a mess." I couldn't tell whether he was talking about the scene in the bedroom or the situation as a whole. Both, probably. "Kirby, what are the odds they'll let you book him in Manhattan?"

"Zero to none," Kirsch said. "Best we can hope for is Monday morning they'll let us move him."

"Monday morning?" I said.

"Look at it this way," Kirsch said. "You're going to spend a weekend in jail, would you rather do it in Flushing or at Midtown South?"

"I'd rather spend it in my own apartment," I said, "or better yet, working on this case, which I can't do if I'm in jail. Look at this. Look." I bent my head forward. "How could I do that to myself?" I pulled him toward the bedroom. "Look at the rug. Someone pulled a trunk through here. If I did it, where's the trunk?"

Lyons' partner was talking into a walkie-talkie the size of a hero roll. Lyons looked up from Lenz's body. "Sir, please calm down."

"I'm calm. I'm just telling you you're arresting me for something I didn't do."

"If you didn't do it, that will come out and you'll be released. In the meantime, we've got you at the scene of a murder with a gun you say is the murder weapon and you're telling us we're going to find your prints on it. Ask the lieutenant there what would happen to us if we didn't book you."

I looked to Kirsch for support and then to Leo, but both knew Lyons was right, and I knew it, too.

"Look, Blake," Kirsch said. "If your story checks out, maybe Monday we can get you cleared."

"That's great, but in the meantime whoever did this has a chance to get away."

Lyons got up and took hold of my arm again. "Let us worry about that, Mr. Blake." He steered me toward the front door.

"Do we have to wait till Monday?" I said. "Doesn't anyone work Saturdays?"

"A Queens judge? On a Saturday?" Kirsch said. "That would take more pull than we've got."

Chapter 21

Booking me took the better part of an hour, and then they took me to an infirmary where a police surgeon washed the back of my head, smeared on some antibiotic ointment, and told me I didn't need stitches. I didn't argue. I had bigger things to worry about than a scar on the back of my head.

They put me in a holding cell with stacked bunks along two walls. One of the bunks was occupied by a man who was shivering. It wasn't cold. The others were empty and I sat on the nearest one.

I wasn't dazed anymore, but I still felt the soreness. It was worse when I lay down, but then I couldn't have slept anyway, not with so much to sort out.

I'd been assuming that Lenz and Miranda had worked alone—or more precisely that they had worked with no one else other than the two burglars Miranda had recruited at the Wildman. But someone had been in Lenz's apartment, had hidden in the bedroom when I'd knocked, and had come out swinging when I'd started pressing Lenz for answers. In principle it didn't have to be someone who'd been in on the robbery—it could just have been a friend who'd jumped to Lenz's defense when it looked like I might shoot him. Except that jumping to someone's defense generally doesn't involve leaving him dead on the floor and walking out with his stash of stolen money.

And the timing was suspicious, too: I didn't get attacked right away, only after Lenz had offered to split the money with me. He hadn't been serious, just desperate—but the friend in the bedroom might have thought Lenz was serious, might at least have thought he was going to talk. This certainly suggested someone with something to hide, someone whose face had gone as pale when I'd threatened to go to Murco as Lenz's had.

Obviously, it had to be someone who knew about the money. Someone Lenz trusted, though he shouldn't have. I thought immediately of Roy—Lenz had presumably been behind it each of the three times Roy came after me, and if Roy was willing to break into a man's apartment on Lenz's say-so, there was obviously more going on there than a simple manager/bouncer relationship. And God knows Roy would be capable of murder. But Roy wouldn't have needed to smash me in the head with a piece of sculpture—a fist would have done fine. And Roy wouldn't have left me alone once I was unconscious. Even if he needed me alive to take the fall for Lenz's murder, he would have gotten in a kick or two.

So who? If I weren't stuck in this cell, I might be able to find out.

"Coffee?"

A cop stood at the bars holding a cardboard deli tray in one hand. I reached through the bars and took one of the cups.

"Think he wants one?" The cop nodded toward my cellmate, who was still twitching in his sleep.

"Not unless you've spiked it with bourbon."

I took the cup back to my bunk. It was barely warm. Hell, it was barely coffee. I couldn't help comparing how the day had started and how it was ending. The smell of fresh-brewed coffee, the feel of Susan's arms around me, her head on my chest—how had I gone from that to this cell stinking of Lysol and sweat? I had a murder charge hanging over my head, a killer slipping further away by the minute, and this cup of brown water that tasted like nothing but would probably keep me up all night if my aching head didn't.

I poured the coffee down the cell's sink, left the cup on the rim, and sat down again. I'd get out. Somehow. But by the time I did, would it be too late? Would Lenz's killer have vanished? Probably. Would I ever find out what had really happened on that rooftop on New Year's Eve? The odds were dropping by the minute.

Come on, Leo, I thought. You can get me out of here.

"You've got a visitor."

It was the same cop who'd brought me the coffee the previous night, looking bleary and eager to get to the end of his shift. But he kept a firm grip on my arm as he led me out of the cell and down the long corridor to one of the station's interview rooms.

I figured it would be Leo, or possibly Susan, or maybe a lawyer Leo had managed to get to come in on a Saturday morning. Or maybe my mother, carrying a cake with a file baked into it. It wasn't.

"Good morning, Mr. Blake," Murco said.

He was by himself, though I imagined the son was probably not far away, maybe waiting in the car outside. He'd dressed for the occasion in a double-breasted suit with a narrow chalk stripe, a shirt with French cuffs, even a handkerchief in the pocket. Classic overcompensation, I thought. The man's trying very hard to show he doesn't belong in here.

His voice didn't suggest any discomfort, though. He spoke quietly and calmly in his hoarse whisper, periodically glancing up over my shoulder through the chicken wire-laced glass at the cop waiting on the other side of the door. "You made the morning news shows," he said. "The papers haven't got it yet, but by tonight they will."

"What are they saying?"

"That you killed my floor manager."

"I didn't."

"Wayne was a valuable employee. Not a perfect one, but he was worth something to me. I can't have people going around killing my employees. Unless, of course, there was a good reason for it in this case."

"I didn't kill him," I said. "I went to his apartment, but someone got behind me and knocked me out. That's who killed him. As for whether whoever did it had a good reason, the answer is yes. Five hundred thousand good reasons."

"You're saying Wayne . . . ?"

"Yes, I'm saying Wayne. He and Miranda worked together to set you up, and then when it looked like you might identify Miranda, he killed her to keep her from talking."

"That's hard for me to believe," he said. "The man had worked for me for years."

"That's probably why he was able to get away with it."

"And who is it you're saying killed him?"

"Not me. That's all I know."

"And the money?"

"Gone," I said. "Whoever killed Lenz has it, presumably, but I'm damned if I know who that is. And as long as I'm locked up in here, I can't find out."

He leaned forward and spoke even more softly than he had until now. "Mr. Blake," he said, "if you weren't locked up in here, would you be able to find my money and the person who took it?"

"If I weren't locked up in here, I could do lots of things," I said. "But I'm being held on a charge of murder."

"If it's true that you didn't do it," he said, "and it's just a matter of their releasing you sooner rather than later . . ." He spread his hands, palms up, as though there were a simple answer to it all. "The police will listen to reason when you talk to them the right way," he said.

"I tried."

"Then you didn't do it the right way."

"Are you saying you can—"

"Let's not talk about what I can do," he said. "What I want to know is what you can do."

Could I give him what he wanted? Maybe. But saying "maybe" wouldn't get me out of jail. "Yes," I said. "I think I can do it."

"You'd better do more than think, Mr. Blake. If I do this for you and you don't come through for me . . ."

Could he really get me out? He seemed confident of it—and given that he'd managed to keep himself out of prison all these years, maybe he had reason for his confidence. I thought about Kirsch's explanation for why they had never booked Murco: he was small potatoes and maybe he'd lead them to someone bigger. Sure, that could be. But maybe this small-potatoes gangster was also making installment payments to the Stan Kirsch Memorial Fund. And maybe he knew the right palms to cross in Queens, too.

Of course, if I accepted this favor and then wasn't able to deliver, I'd wish I was back in my cell with nothing to complain about but bad coffee. But the alternative was worse: sitting in jail while maybe my last chance to find out what had happened to Miranda evaporated.

"Do it," I said.

Whatever Murco did, it worked quickly: I found myself on the steps of the precinct house in less time than it had taken for them to book me in the first place. The cop who gave me back my belt and shoelaces was one I hadn't seen before and he gave me a warning about not leaving town while I was still a material witness in a homicide investigation. I told him I wouldn't dream of it.

An hour later, I climbed out of the train station on Eighteenth Street. I'd tried calling Leo from the train, but couldn't get a clear signal long enough to complete the call; I tried again now and got him.

"Where are you?"

"On my way to the office. I'll be there in a minute."

"How did you—"

"Long story."

"I've been making calls all morning," he said. "But I didn't think I'd gotten anyone to pay attention."

"I got some help from Murco."

"From Murco? Johnny, you don't want his kind of help."

"What I don't want is to be in jail," I said. "And what he's asking for in return happens to be something I want to do anyway."

"Now it is. What about when he asks for something you don't want to do?"

"I'll deal with that then." I hung up as I turned onto our street and whipped out my keys to unlock the door, but Leo beat me to the punch. He looked worse than I did, haggard and rumpled, as though he'd slept in his clothes, if he'd slept at all.

He led me inside and handed me a FedEx package marked for Saturday delivery. "This came this morning. Susan told me you were expecting it."

I looked at the return address: Jacksonville, Florida. This had to be Mo Levy's reluctant contribution. I tore the package open and took out the unlabeled videocassette that was the only thing it contained. Would it be worth watching, I wondered, especially now, when there was so much else I needed to do? What good could it do me to see Miranda and Jocelyn dancing in a video shot three years ago and a thousand miles away?

I almost put it down—I wanted to. But in the end that's what decided it for me. I didn't want to watch the tape because of what I was afraid I might see, and that was a bad reason. I slipped the tape into our VCR, powered up the TV set above it, and pressed Play.

After a minute of snow, a picture jumped into focus. The camerawork was steady, though not otherwise of high quality. I figured Levy had probably hidden a security camera in a light fixture, trained it on the stage, and left it at that. The sound was tinny—I could hear the high notes of the music, but the bass was missing. Of course, sound wasn't what Mo Levy had been most interested in capturing.

Miranda and Jocelyn were already on stage when the video started. They were wearing matching gowns, one red, the other green. They had played up their resemblance to each other with identical haircuts, identical makeup, mirror image moves as they strutted away from each other and back. They moved with self-confidence and the crowd responded. I sat down on the couch, forced myself to keep watching.

They started by playing to the crowd, dancing up to the edge of the stage and back again, bending forward to show lots of cleavage. Then they came together and began working on each other. I watched Miranda stroke Jocelyn's hair, run her fingers along her arms, embrace her from behind. Then they switched, and it was Jocelyn working on Miranda from behind, easing the straps off Miranda's shoulders, peeling the dress away from the lace bra underneath, pulling it down over her hips, holding it while Miranda stepped out. Then it was Miranda's turn, the same moves, till Jocelyn, too, was wearing nothing but heels, a t-back thong, and a push-up bra.

I realized then that they even had the same figure—and why not? They'd probably gone to the same doctor for the surgery, had deliberately told him to give them both the same breasts. It was all part of the act. It was startling how much they managed to looked like each other.

And they were both beautiful. No grotesque caricatures here, no vulgar exaggerations of the female body, just two young women with toned physiques and beautiful faces and more talent for movement than you usually saw on a strip club stage. Or was I just imagining it, trying to paint what I was seeing in the best light I could? The truth was, I couldn't make out all that much. The footage was grainy, the lighting poor. The camera was far enough from the stage that details got lost. As they danced faster and faster, intertwined in each other's arms, I couldn't always keep track of which one was which.

But when they stopped and stood still, caressing each other slowly—then I could tell, then I could see their faces clearly. Miranda was in front. Jocelyn stood behind her, reaching around to slip the clasp of her bra, while Miranda held her pose, hands locked behind her head. And as she stared straight out over the heads of the crowd, straight at the lens of the hidden camera, as Jocelyn opened the bra and pulled the patterned silk away from her breasts and the buzz from the crowd grew louder, I couldn't shake the feeling that Miranda was looking out at me, trying to speak to me, begging for my help.

They changed places. Now it was Miranda's hands on Jocelyn's breasts, baring them for the crowd, and it was Jocelyn looking out at me, staring, as if to say *She's mine now, not yours. Not any more. Not ever again.*

They danced apart and together again, as they had at the start, only now with the room's lights streaking across their bare flesh. They each dropped to their knees one last time, each hooking her thumbs under the strips of fabric at the other's hips, and then even the g-strings were gone. They were in each other's arms now, embracing, kissing each other deeply, and they kept it up until the song finally ended.

They ran offstage while the audience was still cheering, only to be pulled back on a moment later by a man in jeans and a red "Mo's" T-shirt. He had a handheld microphone in one hand and Jocelyn's arm in the other—or was it Miranda's? No, Jocelyn's. He stood between the women, a head shorter than they were, an ugly man grinning lecherously and shouting into his mike, "They're really something, aren't they? Aren't they? *I said, aren't they?*" The crowd roared louder each time he repeated it.

"Then let's hear it for them! Put your hands

together—no, not you, mister, you'd better wipe yours first." Laughter. "Put your hands together for our favorite twins, Randy—"

He raised Miranda's arm over her head like a boxing champion, then turned to the other side and raised Jocelyn's.

"—and Jessie!"

The crowd went wild.

Chapter 22

Randy and Jessie. Our favorite twins.

Why hadn't I seen it? Goddamn it, why? Miranda had danced under the name Randy; *Jocelyn* had been Jessie. If Miranda had kept using the same name after they had split up, why wouldn't Jocelyn?

But if she had—

If she had, it meant Miranda hadn't been the one dancing at the Wildman, the one Matin and the bartender thought they'd recognized from the photo in the paper. It had been Jocelyn. Jocelyn Mastaduno, missing for six years, had been in New York after all, living a stripper's life just a two-hour commute away from her grieving parents and a few miles uptown from where her former partner was dancing.

How had Jocelyn hooked up with Wayne Lenz? God only knew. Maybe she'd danced at the Sin Factory once; maybe Miranda had introduced them. But they'd hooked up somehow, and between the two of them, Lenz and Jocelyn had come up with the plan. It had been Jocelyn who had recruited the burglars, Jocelyn who had walked away with half of Murco's money—and then Jocelyn who had turned to murder to keep it when the burglars were caught and gave her up. Because all the burglars had given—all they could give—was a physical description, and all Jocelyn needed to supply to take the heat off her was a body that matched that description.

It was like one of those optical illusions where first the cubes seem to be pointing in one direction and then suddenly they're pointing in the other, and you can't imagine how they could ever have looked like they weren't. Jocelyn had known that Murco would hunt for her, would eventually find her, and would surely kill her, unless she could get someone else to take the fall. Miranda had not been a perfect match, but she'd been close enough, especially after a pair of hollow point bullets turned her face into what Kirsch had so sensitively described as chopped meat.

Lenz must have broken into Miranda's apartment not to take the money but to plant the torn paper band behind the dresser, so that Murco would know for sure that the dead woman and the woman who'd stolen from him were one and the same. That, and maybe, while he was at it, to remove from the apartment any photos Miranda had of herself that, shown to the folks at the Wildman, might cast some doubt on the point. That would explain why the newspapers hadn't had any recent photos, at least.

Then at midnight on New Year's Eve, it must have been Jocelyn who lured Miranda onto the roof of the Sin Factory, Jocelyn who got behind her and pulled the trigger, Jocelyn who escaped with the murder weapon while Lenz called for the ambulance they both knew could do no harm because it could do no good.

Did I know for sure this was how it had happened? No. Some of the details might be wrong. But the broad outline felt right. It had begun when the girls were teenagers: Jocelyn had lured Miranda to her bed, had talked her into leaving school, had turned her life inside out and remade her into what I had just seen on the video. She had led Miranda step by step down the path that ultimately led to her death, had used her and finally, when it had served her needs, brutally sacrificed her. It was Jocelyn, not Miranda, that had fallen in with thieves and killers. Miranda had just made the fatal mistake of falling in love with a woman who eventually turned into a thief and a killer herself.

Because whether it was Jocelyn or Lenz who had pulled the trigger on the rooftop—and maybe I'd never know—it had to have been Jocelyn who had pulled the trigger in Lenz's apartment. She'd smashed me in the head with Lenz's statue and when he'd gotten out of the chair and headed for the bedroom, she'd picked up my gun and shot him twice, then coolly wheeled a luggage cart filled with a half million dollars past his body and mine, leaving me to take the rap.

Why not kill me, too? Because this way maybe I'd burn in her place for Lenz's murder—and even if I didn't, even if I had the chance to go to Murco as I'd threatened, what could I tell him that would hurt her? As far as Jocelyn knew, I didn't even know she existed. If I told the same story to Murco that I'd told Lenz about Lenz having conspired with Miranda, it did nothing but make Jocelyn's escape cleaner.

Whereas if she'd left Lenz alive and I'd gone to Murco, Murco would have picked him up and he'd have cracked like an egg. He'd almost cracked at my hands, and I hadn't even touched him. And if Lenz gave her up, she'd have been on the run again, only this time with Murco knowing who she was.

It made sense, damn it. All you had to do was look at the world through the eyes of a calculating, soulless bitch who used people and threw them away. I thought about all the interviews Serner had done with the people who had known Jocelyn back in college. They didn't give any hint of this side of her personality. There was no sign that people back then knew what sort of person she really was. But maybe that was the point: no one had known her, or Miranda either, for that matter. And who knows, maybe back then Jocelyn hadn't been so bad—the years on the road, the years spent going from one strip club to the next, must have brought out the worst in her, made her harder and more ruthless, until maybe even Miranda couldn't take it any more and broke up with her. Even though breaking up meant giving up a successful act and starting over, dancing solo at a tenth-rate club like the Sin Factory—maybe it had been worth it for Miranda to get away. But then when Jocelyn had needed Miranda for one last purpose, she had shown up at Miranda's door, flowers in hand, and had talked her into a reconciliation. The reconciliation had been short-lived, and so had Miranda.

So where was Jocelyn now? Gone, along with the money.

But she could be found.

I got up from the couch. Leo was next to me, holding out a bottle and a glass, but I didn't want soothing and I didn't want anything that would calm me down. I wanted blood.

"Damn it, Leo, I know what happened."

"What, just from watching that tape?"

I shrugged my jacket on. "I've got to go."

"Where?"

I yanked open the office door. "We need to find Jocelyn," I said. I raced out into the street. A cab with its light on was passing and I stepped out in front of it to flag it down. I was in and had the door shut before the car could come to a stop.

"You got to be careful," the driver said. "It is very dangerous to run in front of a taxi."

"Just drive." I gave him my mother's address, and when we got there I threw a handful of bills over the back seat. He honked at me as he drove off.

What would Susan have turned up? Something, I prayed. Something that would help us figure out where Jocelyn might have gone. I tapped my foot impatiently as the elevator climbed to the fourteenth floor.

My mother came to the door when I rang and looked startled when she saw me. "My goodness, John, I heard on the news you were arrested—"

"They let me out. Is Susan here?"

"Susan?"

"I'm sorry. Rachel. Is she here?"

"No, she went out. John, what's going on?"

"Where did she go?"

"John Blake, you tell me what's going on or so help me—"

I put one hand on each of her arms. They felt tiny and frail. "Mom, I'm sorry. I can't. Not now. I need to find Rachel. Did she say anything about where she went?"

"Yes, hold on," she said, and picked up a piece of paper from the telephone stand by the door. She took her glasses down from her forehead and squinted at the page. "She's meeting someone at a restaurant. A place called Dorni—" She squinted some more. "Dorneolo? Dormiolo? I can't read what she wrote."

I took the paper from her hand. It said Dormicello.

*

It was early enough in the afternoon that Zen wasn't there yet. Her day-shift bartender was a parolee called Trunks who nodded at me when he saw me come through the door. The place was as close to empty as I'd ever seen it, which was just as well. Less chance for Susan to get herself in a scrape.

She wasn't at the bar or any of the tables out front. There was a wall of booths in the back, past the wall-mounted TV that was quietly showing NY1 and the pool table where a broad-backed guy in a wifebeater blocked my view. I waited till he was between shots and squeezed past, careful not to knock down the second cue stick that was leaning against the table. There was presumably a second player somewhere, maybe in the bathroom, and if he looked anything like this one, I didn't want to do anything to piss him off.

Only one of the booths was occupied, and from where I was I couldn't see who Susan was talking to, just the back of his head. His salt-and-pepper hair was combed straight back and held in place by some sort of shellac, and I had a strong sense of déjà vu: based on his hair alone, he could have been Wayne Lenz's taller, older brother.

I came around to the front of the booth. Susan must have been surprised to see me, but she kept it from showing on her face. "Peter, this is John," she said. "He . . . works with me."

"At the studio?" The man extended his hand. "Good to meet you, John. I'm Pete Cimino."

I shook the hand. "Pete."

"I was explaining to Pete about the segment we're doing for Fox News on the Sugarman murder, and he's offered to help. He's even willing to talk on camera."

On camera. Good God, she was a natural. "That's good, Pete," I said. "Thank you." Susan had her hair tied back and was wearing a simple blouse. She didn't look like a TV producer to me, but she didn't look like a stripper either, and maybe that was enough. People generally believed what you told them, especially when it was something they wanted to believe. And who didn't want to be on TV?

Of course, the answer to that was that most of the people you met at Zen's didn't—but this guy obviously wasn't a regular, not if he called the place Dormicello. He looked like some kind of tough guy wannabe, the sort who thought some hairspray and a Brooklyn accent made him Tony Soprano. If he kept hanging around here, it was just a matter of time before he got on the wrong side of someone who was the real thing and exited with a blade in his stomach. But that was his problem, and Zen's, not ours. He was obviously someone Susan had felt was important enough to meet in person and that meant I wanted to talk to him.

"What do you do, Pete?" I asked.

"Things," he said. "Little of this, little of that. You know how it is."

"And you knew Miranda?"

He kissed his fingertips and sent a glance toward the ceiling.

"What does that mean?" I said.

"May she rest in peace, she was something. A great dancer, and what a body. Really gave a hundred ten percent every night, her and Jessie both. Any time they worked my club, I could make another ten, twelve percent easy, people coming in because of them. When they split up, I tried to talk some sense into them, but no. I even offered them a raise, which I've never done for any girl before or since. But there was no talking to them."

"Why don't you tell John what you were telling me," Susan said. "About how it happened."

He turned to me. "There was this other girl, this black chick, Tracy, who started at the club halfway through their last booking. We used her as their warm-up act. But then things got a little too warm, if you know what I mean."

"I don't," I said.

"Man, this Tracy, I'll tell you, *I* would've done her, and I don't go for no *melanzana* normally. She was built like you wouldn't believe. But strictly a dyke, and she went for Jessie like a bullet. Now, Randy must've known about it from the day it started. She was no dummy. But she didn't say anything, so I figured maybe they've got an agreement, they're not tied down, whatever. Lots of girls are like that. Get so sick of men looking at them, they'll go to bed with anything long as it doesn't have a dick." He raised a placating hand to Susan. "Excuse my French."

"You can say 'dick' in here," Susan said, "just not on the air."

"So this goes on for two weeks, three weeks. It's coming up on the end of their booking, and I'm thinking I want them to extend—all three of them, what the hell, the guys love Tracy, too. So I go to talk to them backstage and it's like walking into a meat locker. They're not talking to each other. They're glaring at each other like they're ready to take each other's eyes out. It was ugly."

"And?"

He shrugged. "What can I tell you? I tried to get them to talk, I tried to joke with them a little, but they weren't having any of it. If it got to the point where I offered money, you know it was bad."

"What makes you think they broke up because of Tracy?"

"It was obvious. All three of them were there, and every time Tracy moved closer to Jessie, Randy moved further away. It was like two magnets, you know, pushing each other apart? Finally, Tracy put her arm around Jessie and Randy just walked out. That was it. Never came back."

"What about Jessie?" I asked.

"She re-upped for two more weeks, tried to teach Tracy the act, but it wasn't the same. You know, black and white's not twins, and the twin angle was part of what had made it so hot. But the real problem was just they weren't good together. They may have been great in the sack, but onstage? There wasn't that chemistry. They were easy on the eyes, but you put the two of them on stage and it was just two strippers on a stage. With Randy it was something else."

I'd seen what it had been, and he was right. There'd been something more between them. I tried to imagine the backstage scene Cimino had described, thought about what it must have been like for Miranda to find herself suddenly cast off and replaced in Jocelyn's life by this other woman. This, after giving up her dreams of medical school and spending years traveling the country at Jocelyn's side. It must have been crushing.

"When did this happen?"

"What, a year ago? Year and a half, maybe."

"And you had no idea where Miranda went after she left?"

"None. Not till you guys called me."

"Do you know what happened to the other two? Jessie and Tracy?"

"I think they were living together for a while. Then they broke up. You know how it goes. I think Tracy's dancing somewhere in the city. I haven't heard from Jessie in ages. Maybe Tracy would know how to find her."

Maybe she would. "How could we find Tracy?"

Susan spoke up. "Pete gave me the number of her booking agent, a guy named Andrew Kodos. I have a call in to him."

"Good," I said. "Well, Pete, I think that covers it. You've been very helpful." I stood up, and Susan stood with me.

"So?" he said. "You think you'll be able to use me?"

"There's an excellent chance," Susan said. "We'll let you know."

"You'll call me?" he said, miming a phone receiver with his thumb and pinky.

"We'll call you," I said.

We backed away toward the pool table. Out of the corner of my eye, I saw there were two guys there now, but instead of playing, they were watching the TV. As we passed them, I realized the story being covered was the Lenz murder: the newscaster was standing across the street from the Sin Factory and the picture framed in a box over his shoulder showed Lenz's face next to mine. ". . . sources have informed us that the only suspect in the shooting, private investigator John Blake, was released from custody earlier today. Police say they are investigating other leads, but so far they haven't released any further information. We'll be updating the story as soon as they do. Pat?"

The two pool players watched us closely as we walked past them, then they both leaned their cues against the table and one stepped forward, the taller of the two. It

was the one who'd been in the bathroom earlier, and he
looked like he benchpressed more than I weighed.

"Hey," he said. "You're the guy they were talking
about."

I shrugged, turned to go, but a hand on my shoulder
stopped me. "Go on," I said to Susan, "I'll handle this."

"I'm not going to—"

"Go." I pushed the big man's hand off my shoulder
with the back of my arm. "Why don't we each mind our
own business?"

"Wayne Lenz and I did time together," he said, clapping his hand back where it had been. "Who killed him is
my business."

"Mine, too," I said, "and if you leave me alone I might
be able to find out."

"He might be able to find out," he said over his
shoulder to his buddy. "You hear that?" He looked back
at me, and there was no trace of sympathy in his voice.
"You want to give me one good reason why I shouldn't
just break your fucking neck?"

From behind the bar came the sound of a pump-
action shotgun being racked. Trunks leveled the long
barrel at the lot of us. "Take it outside," he said.

The hands lifted from my shoulders and the guy gave
me a little push that rocked me back on my heels.
"Private investigator," he said, in a voice that suggested
he thought private investigators fell somewhere between
worms and dogshit on the evolutionary scale. "Why don't
you investigate this?" He reached back with one of his
big fists, and I put up my own smaller ones to block him.

"*Outside,*" Trunks barked, and gestured with the gun.

"Hello?" Susan had taken out her cell phone and was
speaking into it loudly, pointedly, staring Lenz's old cellmate in the eyes as she did. We were all watching her—

even Pete Cimino was watching from his booth in the back. "I want to report gunfire coming from a place called Dormicello— Yes, officer, west Third Street, that's right. Please send someone immediately."

The guy looked from Susan to me, to Trunks, and back again. She didn't blink. "The cops will be here in a minute," she said.

He stepped back, dropped his fists, angrily picked up his cue stick. "Next time," he said.

We didn't turn our backs on him, and Trunks kept the gun up till we were at the door.

Chapter 23

"You didn't really call the police, did you?" I said.

"Of course I did. Those guys could have killed you."

"You called the police on Zen's," I said. "I can never show my face in there again."

She patted my cheek. "Well, then, honey, we're even."

We walked away from Zen's as quickly as we could. Trunks could take care of himself—he'd have a good hiding place for the gun, and maybe one for himself, too. As for Zen, she might forgive me in time, depending on how badly the police shook her down. The police, though, were unlikely to be as forgiving, so it was important that they not find me at yet another scene where shooting had been reported.

We headed east, putting the sound of police sirens further behind us with every step. As we went, I told Susan about my morning, about getting out of jail and watching the video, and about what I figured Jocelyn had done.

"It's hard to believe," she said. "Nothing I've heard makes her sound like the sort of person who could turn into a murderer."

"Anyone could," I said. "If they thought their life depended on it."

"I guess."

"Have you learned anything that would help us track her down?"

"Only what Cimino told us. I've made a lot of calls, and I've found some people who remember Miranda and Jocelyn, but no one who worked with them more recently than Cimino."

"Where does he work?"

"He runs a club called Shots down on Houston."

"I don't know it. What's it like?"

"It's not Scores. You don't get your Charlie Sheens and your Howard Sterns going there. But it's a lot higher on the food chain than Carson's or the Sin Factory."

"Have you ever worked there?"

She shook her head. "It's a little out of my league."

"Miranda danced there."

"Sure, when she was doing her act with Jocelyn. That was a hot act. After they broke up, she wasn't so hot any more. She had to work the same places as the rest of us."

"See, that's what I don't understand," I said. "You're a beautiful woman, you're a good dancer—"

"I hear a 'but' coming," she said.

"No, no 'but.' It's just that I don't understand why—and please don't take this the wrong way—but what I don't understand is why someone like you or Miranda would need to work at a place like the Sin Factory. It's such a dump—it's small, it's dark, it's a rotten place. The managers are crooks. You should be able to find work at better clubs."

"I do," she said, only sounding a little defensive. "Sometimes. Some of the places I work at are better. Some are worse. But you've got to work. You know? After you've been doing this for a while, you learn not to be so choosy. Every place has spotlights, they've all got stages and poles and guys who grab your ass, the managers are always crooks—so one night you're here, the next you're there, does it really matter where 'here' and 'there' are?"

"Of course it matters," I said. "It matters whether you've got ten guys watching you or a hundred—"

"No, see, because the places where you've got a hundred, you've also got ten times as many girls. You can make less money at the bigger clubs."

"Okay, but the tips—the guys at the Sin Factory were laying down ones and fives. I think I saw one twenty once."

"Yeah, Mandy's guy. He came every night." Susan stopped to catch her breath. I glanced around, but no one I saw looked like they were paying attention to us. "The truth is, John, fives add up. Even ones do. Yes, twenties are better. I won't lie to you, I didn't like working at the Sin Factory. But you take what you can get. There are only so many good clubs—most of what's out there isn't so good. But you've got to eat every night, not just a couple of times a week, and there are a lot of girls out there who'll take the jobs if you don't. Ones and fives are a lot better than nothing, and if you start turning down gigs, that's what you end up with pretty soon—nothing."

"I'm sorry," I said. "I didn't mean to pry."

"Yes you did. But that's okay. It's your job, prying." We started walking again. "Speaking of which, you know, it's not like your job is a whole lot better."

Why did it hit me so hard? It was nothing but the truth. Who the hell was I to ask her why she worked for tenth-rate clubs when I was working for a twentieth-rate detective agency?

"No, it's not," I said. "You're right."

"So there you go. You work where you work and I work where I work. Maybe we both deserve better, but we take what we can get. That's all I'm saying. We're not in such different positions."

"You know what the difference is?" I said. "The man I work for? I'd trust him with my life."

"Yeah, well," Susan said. "You've got me there."

"Maybe you should try that agent again," I said, but she was already dialing.

"Busy," she said. She closed the phone.

"At least that's a good sign. Means he's there."

"Or that someone else was leaving a message for him."

"We'll try again in a few minutes," I said.

We turned uptown, headed toward Ninth Street. "If you were Jocelyn," I said, "where would you go?"

"If I had half a million dollars in stolen money and a couple of killers coming after me?"

"She may not think they're still coming after her."

"I would, if I were her."

"Okay," I said. "A couple of killers coming after her."

"And you."

"And me."

She thought for a second and then shook her head. "I don't know. We don't even know where she lives. She might go there. She might go back to Tracy, depending on how things ended between them. She might have some other girlfriend, or boyfriend. She could rent a hotel room."

"Or she could get on a plane and fly to Peru," I said. "All true. But what would *you* do if you were her?"

"Me?" She thought for a second. "I'd go home."

"Even though you could be traced there?"

"I might not stay there, but I'd go there. That's where all my stuff is, I can crash there, get my bearings. It's where I'd feel safest."

She'd go home. It made a certain amount of sense. But where was home for Jocelyn? Unfortunately, we had no idea. I didn't even know where home was for Susan, for God's sake.

It suddenly struck me that Susan's address was the least of what I didn't know about her—I still didn't know her last name, for instance.

"Susan," I said, "this may sound strange, but—"

"What?"

"What does the 'F' stand for?" I held up my cell phone. "Susan F."

"That's okay. It's not strange," she said. "It stands for Feuer. F-E-U-E-R. My dad's family was German. Mom was French-Canadian, but you wouldn't know it from her name, which was Stine."

"Feuer-Stine," I said. "Firestone."

"Give the man a cigar."

"Where did you get Rachel?"

"I just liked it. Susan is so plain-Jane. I always wanted something more exciting."

"I think Susan is pretty exciting," I said.

She took my hand, squeezed it. "Listen," she said, "I know how this goes. Next you'll want to know where I live, and how I got into stripping, and what was my childhood like, and you know what, maybe one of these days I'll want to share all that with you, but not today, okay?"

"Okay."

She squeezed my hand again.

"So, who could tell us where Jocelyn lives?" I asked. "Did she have an agent?"

"Not according to Cimino. He said she and Miranda handled their own bookings."

"Have you heard about any friends they had?"

She waved her phone. "This Tracy is the first I've heard about."

"Relatives?"

"Nobody mentioned any."

"There's her parents, but if she hasn't seen them in six years, I don't see her going back to them now."

"Probably not."

"But maybe?" I said. "I guess it's worth checking." I pulled up my phone's menu of incoming calls, scrolled back to the last call I'd received from Daniel Mastaduno. "Why don't you try Kodos again?" She was dialing when I heard Daniel pick up.

"Mr. Mastaduno, this is John Blake—"

"Have you found anything?" I heard the eagerness in his voice and I knew there was no good news. He wouldn't sound like that if she'd come back.

"No, I'm afraid not. I was hoping you might have."

"Me?"

"We believe Jocelyn was in New York recently, and we thought there was a slim chance she might have gotten back in touch with you."

"No, Mr. Blake, she hasn't. I have a feeling her mother and I are the last people she'd get in touch with."

"I'm sorry," I said. "If you do hear anything, though, will you please give me a call?"

"Of course," he said. "But Mr. Blake—I wouldn't wait for it."

"No," I said. "I won't."

I hung up and turned to Susan. "Nothing," I said. "You?"

She held up one hand. " . . . four o'clock? That's fine. Eighth floor, I've got it. Thanks. See you then." She was smiling as she closed her phone. "I got him," she said. She sounded excited. It reminded me of how I'd been when I started working for Leo, when each small success had felt like a major triumph. "I told him we'd heard about Tracy and wanted to hire her for a new club we're opening in the West Village. He said she was booked through the end of February, so I said that was fine, we weren't opening till March, but we'd want to talk to her now, and he said okay, she'd be in his office later today anyway, we could come by."

"That's terrific."

"This detective stuff isn't so hard," she said. "Maybe we should trade jobs."

"I'd look lousy in a g-string."

"Oh, I don't know," she said.

The doorman waved us past when we got to my mother's building, then came running up to us before we could get in the elevator. He held out an envelope with nothing but "14-A" written on it. "I forgot. Someone dropped this off for you."

"For me?"

"Yeah, a woman. Asked me to give it to you."

"What did she look like?"

He shrugged. "Dressed up warm. Winter coat, hat, earmuffs, scarf, sunglasses. Couldn't see much of her face, to tell you the truth."

"And she said to give this to me?"

"You're John, right? Margaret Blake's son?" I nodded. "Well, that's who she said to give it to."

"Thanks."

I waited till the elevator door closed, then tore the envelope open. I read the single piece of paper inside and passed it to Susan.

In plain type on a sheet of plain paper it said, *Stop looking for me, or you'll be sorry.*

Chapter 24

"How could she know about this apartment?" Susan asked.

"I don't know. Maybe she followed us."

"From where?"

"I don't know!" I tried to get my voice under control. "Maybe one of the people you called is still friendly with her and passed her this phone number. She could have looked up the address in a reverse directory—"

"But I didn't leave this number anywhere," Susan said.

"Then I don't know." I finished checking the windows in the living room—they were all locked. Not that it mattered when you were fourteen stories up, but somehow it made me feel a little less uncomfortable. I pulled the blinds down.

"How she found out doesn't really matter," I said. "What matters is that she did. I can't leave my mother alone now. Or you, for that matter."

"I can take care of myself."

"How, if you're on the street and she comes up to you with a gun, or a knife?"

"Me? What about you?"

"I have to go after her," I said. "You don't."

"What are you talking about? I'm part of this now. You made me part of it, remember?"

I took her hand. "You are part of it, and I can't tell you how grateful I am. Without you, there's no way we'd be this close. But your part is back here on the phone, not on the street. I can't watch out for both of us."

"Why can't we watch out for each other?"

"You could get hurt or killed. It's bad enough that I have to run that risk—you don't." She looked like she was getting ready to argue. "Anyway, I need you here. I need you to keep making calls. And I need to you watch out for my mother. Jocelyn could show up here at any time, and if she does, I need you to call me, call Leo, call the police—whatever you do, just don't face her alone. This is a woman who's already killed two people. Four, if you count the burglars she set up. We just can't take any chances."

"What about our appointment with Tracy? They're expecting me."

"I'll go. I'll tell them I'm your partner."

She shook her head, but what she said was, "Okay, John. I'm not brave. I'll stay here, and you can get the bruises for the both of us."

"It's not bruises I'm worried about this time," I said.

"So why don't you stay here, too? We can talk to Tracy on the phone."

"And then what? Corner Jocelyn on the phone, too? Talk her into giving herself up?"

We watched each other. "Just be careful," Susan said finally. "If something happened to you—" She broke off, embarrassed.

I went into my mother's bedroom. My mother was sitting on the edge of her bed, looking more annoyed than frightened, but I could see a little of each in her eyes.

"Mom," I said, "please listen to Rachel while I'm out. No matter what, you've got to stay in the apartment. I'm sorry about this, but you won't be safe otherwise."

"Why not?"

"We got a threat from the woman we're trying to track down. She knows about this apartment, and if she has a chance, she might do something to you."

"To me? I'm an old woman. Why would she want to hurt me?"

"She doesn't, she just wants me to stop looking for her, and she figures threatening you might get me to do it."

"So why don't you? Why don't you let Leo handle it?"

"This is the woman who killed Miranda," I said. "I have to handle it."

She seemed to accept that, grudgingly. "How long will this go on?" she said

"Not long," I said. "I think we're getting pretty close."

Andrew Kodos had a suite in an old skyscraper on Forty-second and Lex. Beautiful Art Deco carvings on the outside of the building, soaring lobby, but by the time you got up to the eighth floor, you weren't surprised any more that a guy who booked strippers for a living worked here. The hallway was poorly lit and dingy. At one end, a mop and bucket had been abandoned. There was a locked men's room and a women's room whose door was propped open with a block of wood. In between were five doors advertising five separate businesses. This being Saturday, all but one of the doors were dark.

The one with light behind it said "Kodos Theatrical Representation" in gold letters on the pebbled glass. I wondered if his theatrical work involved handling anyone other than strippers. But I knew the choice of wording was probably just to avoid spooking the building management. It was the same reason Leo had finally settled on "Hauser Consulting Services" for our door.

I pressed the button by the doorknob, then knocked on the glass when I didn't hear anything buzzing or chiming. I saw a shadow approach through the glass. The door swung open. "Come in, come in." Kodos looked behind me, saw no one else in the hall, and shut the door.

He was a well-fed specimen, extra pounds pressing the limits of his belt, which was straining at its last hole, and his shirt collar, which looked tight even unbuttoned. A blue necktie hung at half-mast, knotted but loosened as far as it would go. He wiped his hand on the leg of his pants before extending it to me but when I shook it his palm still felt damp against mine.

"You spoke to my partner earlier today," I said. "We're opening a club downtown."

"Sure, I remember. It's good to meet you. Where's your partner?"

"Something came up at the last minute," I said. "She's sorry she couldn't come."

"Me, too. She sounded like a good-looking young woman." He coughed into his hand. "Excuse me. Every January I get a cold. Like clockwork. So where's this club of yours going to be?"

What had Susan said, the West Village? "You know where Calder Street is, near the West Side Highway?" Fortunately, it looked like he didn't. "That's where we'll be."

"And how'd you hear about Tracy?"

"I didn't, my partner did. You'd have to ask her."

"Well, you won't be disappointed. She's the best." He

led me through a short corridor lined on either side with framed eight-by-tens of women in all sorts of outfits: stockings and garters, boas and headdresses, bikinis and evening gowns. You could tell from the hairstyles that some of the photos went back to the eighties, some to the seventies. There were even a few black-and-white shots that looked older still. Many of the photos were signed: *To Andy, the greatest agent in the world! Love, Cherry.* Or *Asia*, or *Crystal*, or *Jet*.

"How long have you been doing this?" I asked.

"Signed my first girl in 1962," he said, pointing to a photo. "Maxine Murray. Danced under the name 'Sissy.' Can you imagine a dancer calling herself 'Sissy' now?" He shook his head at the wonder of the world. "That was before you were even born. How old are you anyway?"

"Old enough," I said.

"Aren't we all." He opened the door to his office. "Tracy, I want you to meet—" He waited for me to fill in my name.

"John Blake," I said. I held my hand out and she leaned forward in her seat to shake it. She could have stood up, but that wouldn't have given me a view of her breasts pressing forward against the front of her scoop neck T-shirt. It was a thin shirt and her dark skin showed through the white fabric. I could see that she was wearing small rings through her nipples. If I'd looked closer, I could probably have told whether they were silver or gold.

"Andy, would you mind if I talked to Tracy alone for a minute?"

He looked puzzled, but he said, "Sure. Sure." Then he told Tracy, "He's opening a club down on . . . where was it?"

"Calder Street," I said.

"Calder Street. And they want you for the opening. I told him you'd be perfect for it."

"Did you?" she said. But she was looking at me rather than at Kodos, and somewhere along the way it had turned into a skeptical look. I wondered what I'd said or done wrong.

"So, you kids talk. Just don't forget to bring me back in before you talk money." He patted me on the shoulder. "That desk folds out into a bed in case you need it." Then, to Tracy, "What? What? I'm joking!" He backed out of the office and drew the door shut behind him. I waited for his silhouette to disappear.

"Tracy—"

"You're not really opening a club, are you?" she said.

I hesitated for a second, then shook my head.

"Then, if it's all the same to you, I think I'll put my shirt back on." She pulled a folded flannel shirt from under the chair and buttoned it up over her T-shirt.

"What gave me away?" I said.

She held up a fist and unfolded fingers from it one by one. "First of all, I've never seen a club owner or manager who looked like you. You look like some prep school kid from the Upper West Side. Second, Calder Street's two blocks long and there's a church on one of them. No way the city's going to let you open a titty bar where the faithful might have to look at it. Third, I seem to remember a friend of mine telling me about a John Blake who was passing out business cards to the girls at the club where she works, asking questions about Miranda Sugarman. As it happens, I knew Miranda Sugarman."

"I know."

"So the name stuck in my mind. John Blake. I may even have your card in here somewhere." She lifted a handbag that was hanging from one arm of the chair.

"That's okay. I'll give you a new one." I fished one out of my wallet. She looked at it, slipped it into the breast pocket of her lumberjack shirt.

"So, you want to tell me why you're wasting my time on this beautiful Saturday afternoon?"

"I guess you know I'm a private detective. My firm's been looking into Miranda's death. I understand you knew her partner, too. Jocelyn Mastaduno."

"That's right."

"Well, we're trying to find her. Do you have any idea where Jocelyn is now?"

"Why?"

"We think she might know something about what happened."

"Know something like what?"

"Like what happened."

Tracy folded her arms over her chest. "You'd better start talking straight, or I'm walking out that door."

"Miranda was killed by two gunshots fired at close range into the back of her head. The person who did it had to be someone who was able to get close to her, someone Miranda trusted."

"You think *Jocelyn* killed her?"

"It's one possibility. We'd like to rule it out."

"No way," she said. "I'm not saying I can't imagine Jocelyn doing something crazy—the girl had her issues. But there's no way she would kill Miranda. She was still in love with her."

"Why do you say that?"

"Because she was. She couldn't go two nights without mentioning her name. She kept her fucking picture up on the wall. Even after I moved in, she wouldn't take it down."

"You lived with her?"

"Not for long. I don't mind the occasional three-way, but I'm not competing with some girl's not even there. And Jocelyn was a little too crazy for me—too needy, too high strung. But none of that makes her a killer."

"No, it doesn't," I said. "But if she didn't do it, someone's gone to a lot of trouble to make it look like she did. She might be in danger herself, frankly. I'd at least like to talk to her, get her side of the story."

She closed her eyes, leaned her head back. "Don't bullshit me. You think she did it."

I didn't say anything for a while and neither did she.

"Yes," I said. "I do."

"When Miranda moved out, Jocelyn had the apartment all to herself, and she asked me to stay with her, so I moved in. You know how long it lasted? Two months. I couldn't take it. Every word out of her mouth was Miranda this and Miranda that, and did I think she'd call, and what should she say if she did. It was like they were a married couple and I was just some one-night stand Jocelyn had hooked up with."

"The way you describe it, I'm surprised it lasted two months."

"Me, too," she said. "But when you're in the middle of it, you always think you're going to be able to make it work. The problem is, someone like Jocelyn, there's just no way. She needed to get Miranda out of her system, but she couldn't."

That sounded like a perfect recipe for murder to me, even if you didn't take the circumstances of the burglary into account. But I didn't say so. "When was the last time you saw her?"

"Been close to a year now. I called her once after I moved out, but she never called back."

"Do you think she's still living in the same apartment?"

"I have no idea. Probably."

"Where is it?"

"Down in Alphabet City, near the water," she said.

"You remember the address?"

"Before I answer that," she said carefully, "I want to know what you're going to do with it."

"I'm going to go talk to her. That's all." She stared at me and I held her eyes.

"I don't believe you," she said.

"For God's sake, Tracy—you want it straight? I'll give it to you straight. It's not just Miranda that's dead. Four people are dead because of Jocelyn. I don't know for sure whether she shot Miranda, but I do know she shot a man named Wayne Lenz yesterday."

"How do you know that?"

"Because I was there." I bent my head forward. "She gave me this. Hit me with a heavy statue so hard it shattered, then took my gun and used it to kill a man she'd been working with."

She was silent.

"And that's not the half of it. There's a drug dealer involved, and even if I drop the case right now, he's not going to, because she's got a half million dollars of stolen money that he wants back. Do you understand, Tracy? She's in way over her head. I know you want to protect her, but you can't."

"That doesn't mean I have to help you find her," she said.

"No, it doesn't. And I'm sure you'll be glad you didn't help me if she decides to come after you."

"What are you talking about?"

"There are professional killers looking for her. The only thing keeping her alive is her anonymity. You know where she lives, you know what she looks like—why *wouldn't* she come after you?"

She started to say something, then stopped herself. I waited her out. "She's just a screwed-up girl," she said. "She's not a killer."

"And I'm telling you she is. Are you willing to bet your life on it?"

I waited some more while she wrestled with her decision.

"Hell with it," she said finally. "It's the top floor apartment at 51 Avenue D. Facing the street."

"Thank you," I said. I got up and walked to the door.

"You won't tell her I gave you the address, will you?"

"No, I won't."

"And what are you going to tell Andy?"

"I'll tell him I think you're perfect, then I'll call him next week and tell him the financing fell through, the club's not going to open after all. That way he won't blame you."

"Fine." She sounded sullen, or maybe just disgusted with herself. Or with me.

"Listen, Tracy, I'm sorry about using a ruse to get you in here. I wish I did have a job to give you."

"Oh, you gave me a job," she said. "You just didn't pay me my thirty pieces of silver for doing it."

Chapter 25

If you read the *Village Voice*, it sounds like Alphabet City has become hopelessly gentrified over the past ten years, all the quaint, stoop-sitting crackheads and heroin addicts replaced with Starbucks junkies out for a double latte. It's only true up to a point. I still wouldn't want to be caught east of Avenue C after dark.

But that's where I was headed, and the sky wasn't getting any lighter. In the summer you'd see guys with boomboxes hanging out till eight, nine at night, and though you knew some of them were up to no good, you also knew some of them were just enjoying what passed for fresh air in this part of town. You'd see some women on the streets, too, and not only hookers. You didn't get the feeling that all the honest people were locked up indoors, leaving the streets to the predators. But it was not summer now, and in the winter the combination of the early darkness and the bone-chilling cold kept everyone off the streets who had someplace better to go.

I didn't. I had one place to go and only one, and it was on Avenue D, as far east as you could walk before you hit the waterfront housing projects, the FDR Drive, and then the East River itself. The wind blew harder as you got closer to the water. There were few tall buildings here to block it, mostly just red brick tenements and little Spanish churches. When the wind came from the east, you could smell the river on it. It stank of diesel fuel.

I wasn't the only one on the streets, but in some ways I'd have preferred it if I had been. I passed two young men walking together, and we all eyed each other as we passed. It was at times like this that I wished I looked older, bigger, harder. Tracy wasn't so far off with her description, and this was not a neighborhood for slumming prep school kids.

I crossed Avenue C and walked east on Sixth Street, where the concentration of churches was highest. Iglesia Cristiana, Abounding Grace, Emmanuel Presbyterian, all on one block—it was a little safer, I figured, than the blocks on either side. But then the churches were behind me and the avenue I turned onto had nothing warm and welcoming on it. A few bodegas, some shuttered with metal gates, some open behind grimy windows. One Chinese restaurant. There were two men in khaki jackets transacting some business under the awning of what had once been a butcher shop and now had a big "Store for Rent" sign in the window. The one who pocketed the money fell into step beside me as I passed.

"Smoke, smoke," he muttered under his breath—though why he bothered to keep quiet, I don't know. There wasn't a cop for blocks around.

"No, thanks." I shook his fingers off my sleeve.

"Come on, man. I've got good shit."

"I'm sure you do. I'm not buying."

"That's cool, man. How about just helping a brother out, cold night like this." He had a hand out, and I was tempted to give him something just to make him go away, but that was a path I knew better than to go down. Not because he was a drug dealer—the hell with that. Just because once I took anything out of my pocket, he'd want whatever else I had in there.

"Sorry," I said. "Try someone else."

"No," he said, and suddenly his voice wasn't so quiet any more, "how about I try you, motherfucker?" He whipped something out of his jacket pocket, and I heard the click-click of a butterfly knife swinging open. Butterfly knives are illegal in New York, but then so are drug deals and muggings. If there had been a cop around, I could have had this guy booked for all three.

I held my palms up. "Don't do this."

"Shut the fuck up and give me your wallet." He gestured with the knife. It was a short blade, only four inches or so, but you can do plenty of damage with a short blade. Simon Corrina had always used a knife like this.

I looked around, but there was no one in sight. The guy who'd made a buy just a minute ago had vanished, and I didn't blame him.

I reached into my pocket for my wallet, held it out to him. I thought about flipping it open and showing him my license, but I wasn't sure whether that would get me my wallet back or a knife in the guts.

He snatched it. "Come on, come on," he said. "What else you got?"

He reached under my jacket to pat down my pockets. He found my cell phone in its holster on my hip, popped it out, and slipped it into his own pocket. He slapped my right pants pocket. "What's that?"

"Just my keys," I said. "You don't want my keys, man. Come on."

"Show me."

I pulled out the keyholder, opened it for him. He gestured with the knife. "Okay." I put it back. "Give me your watch."

"I don't wear a watch," I said.

"Bullshit," he said. "This can't be all you've got."

"I'm sorry," I said. "It is."

We both heard a buzzing sound then. It started quiet and got louder. He looked down toward his pocket, and so did I, but only for a second. Before he could look back, I stepped in, braced his knife hand with one forearm, put my other hand around his throat and ran him back against the wall of the building next to us. He swung at me with his free hand, but it was a weak punch and I blocked it with my elbow. I hammered his head against the wall until his grip on the knife loosened and it fell to the sidewalk, and then a few more times just because it felt good. I brought my knee up, aiming for his crotch, but got his stomach instead. He folded up all the same. I let go of him and he collapsed on the pavement. I kicked the knife out of his reach and then squatted next to him to go through his pockets. I found my wallet and phone in one and some loose bills and a baggie full of plastic vials in the other. The phone had stopped buzzing. I took it all, rolled him into the doorway of the butcher shop, and left him there.

I shoved the baggie deep into the garbage can on the corner. The butterfly knife was lying in the gutter, so I picked it up, folded it shut, and pocketed it. Now I was the one breaking the law, but what the hell. It probably wouldn't be the last time tonight. I checked the readout of my phone, but all it said was "Missed Call— Unavailable." Well, there was nothing I could do. If it was important, whoever it had been would call back.

I crossed to the next block and checked building numbers till I found 51. It was a grey stone building with a fire escape zigzagging down the front. The windows were all dark, and on the ground floor some were boarded up. I didn't see any intercom buttons next to the front door, which said something about how old this building was— it must have been from the throw-the-key-down era. I looked up at the top-floor apartment. Was Jocelyn in there? If she were, I thought, the lights would be on— she wouldn't be asleep at five o'clock, and she wouldn't be sitting in the dark, either. Or would she? She might if she knew I was coming. But how could she know? Tracy wouldn't have called her—would she?

Of course, all of this assumed she had come back here at all. Just because Susan thought that was what she would do in Jocelyn's place, it didn't mean Jocelyn had actually done it. The most likely case was that the apartment was dark because it was empty, and that it was empty because Jocelyn knew better than to come here.

There was only one way to find out. I jumped for the bottom rung of the fire escape ladder. On my second try, the ladder slipped its hook and clattered down. I pulled myself up and started climbing. At the first landing, I crouched between the two windows to catch my breath. I figured the noise would draw some attention, but the street was empty now and none of the windows around me flew open, no angry tenant stuck his head out to see what the racket was. I climbed up to the second landing, and then slowly, working hard not to make any noise, went on to the third. I felt very conspicuous. It wasn't broad daylight, but anyone who happened to look this way would spot me. Who knew what neighbor might be calling the police right now to report what they were seeing? But I kept going.

The top floor was next, and I took each step gently on the way up. The window on my right looked into a bedroom, the one on my left into a kitchen, and I dodged away quickly after risking a glance through each. Both rooms were dark and looked empty. I tried raising the bedroom window, but it was locked. I opened the blade of the butterfly knife and slipped it between the upper and lower panes, forced the latch of the lock sideways, then shifted the blade to the bottom and used it to lever the window up enough to give me a fingerhold on the frame. I slid the window all the way up, climbed inside, and pulled it down behind me.

The room was empty, all right—but at some point recently it hadn't been. On the queen-sized bed a crumpled comforter was pushed to one side. And on a table next to the bed there was a quarter-full glass of water.

I kept the knife ready as I slid the closet door open,

but there was no one waiting inside to jump out at me. No one was in the living room either, or the bathroom when I quickly looked inside. The apartment was empty. I was tempted to turn on a light, but that would have been crazy—I didn't know when Jocelyn would be back, and if she saw the light from the street, she'd know someone was there. I went back into the bedroom and gave it a more thorough once-over. The room's one dresser was nearly empty and so was the closet—lots of empty wire hangers and drawers with only a shirt or two in them. It looked like Jocelyn was planning a quick departure.

I was about to close the closet when I noticed something on the floor in the back behind the sliding door. I pulled it out to get a better look at it. It was a wheeled luggage cart, lying on its back, unzipped and open, crammed full of clothing. It was too dark to see anything on the hard rubber wheels, but I had a feeling I knew what the police would find if they scraped them. Wayne Lenz's blood.

I pawed through the clothing, but that was all the luggage contained, all the way to the bottom: T-shirts, underwear, two pairs of shoes, some costumes of the sort I'd seen on the video and in Miranda's apartment. There was a small cosmetics bag, but it contained nothing but cosmetics. There was no sign of the money.

Not that Jocelyn would be likely to leave five hundred thousand dollars in cash lying around in the closet of a tenement apartment. I tried to guess how much space that much money would take up. About as much as two reams of typing paper, maybe three, even if you packed it tightly. I went through the luggage again, felt around the bottom of the closet, glanced under the bed.

It was disappointing, but only slightly. The money was

why Murco was after her, and if it didn't turn up he would be very unhappy, but otherwise it meant nothing to me. What I was after was Jocelyn. I wanted to hear her admit what she had done, and then—

And then what? I felt my hand tighten around the knife. And then I'd call the police, damn it. And then I'd have her arrested, have them test the luggage, have them clear my name and put her in jail where she belonged. There was a part of me that ached for a rawer sort of justice, the sort Murco and his son would deal out—part of me felt Miranda deserved that sort of retribution. But I was not Murco. Justice didn't have to come at the point of a knife.

I pushed the luggage back into place and drew the closet door in front of it. I went back into the living room, searched through the small pile of mail I found on a table. A clothing catalogue, a credit card bill, a belated Christmas card, all addressed to "Jessie Masters." I left them where they were.

There was an answering machine on the table, showing one message on its digital readout. I pressed the Play button and heard a woman's voice. It took me a second to realize whose it was.

"Hey, beautiful," Miranda said. "It was really good seeing you again. I know it was strange for you. For me, too. But I'd like to do it again, okay? Maybe we could watch the fireworks tomorrow. We should be able to see them from where I'm working. Maybe we can get some dinner first, before I have to go on. Give me a call, okay? Or I'll call you, if you don't." Pause. "I love you, you know." The machine clicked. A mechanical voice said, "Received Friday, December 30, at seven thirty-four p.m."

She sounded so eager, so happy. Why? Why had Miranda been so trusting, so willing to take Jocelyn's overtures at face value, so quick to forgive? I pictured Jocelyn getting this message and laughing, unable to believe her good luck. *We should be able to see them from where I'm working.* She hadn't even had to come up with some excuse to lure Miranda to a secluded spot. New Year's Eve meant fireworks on the Hudson, and sure, maybe you could see them from the roof at the Sin Factory—it was a short building, but it was far enough west that at least you'd see some of the show over the tops of other buildings. And how hard would it have been for Jocelyn to get behind Miranda while they were both watching the show, press the gun to the back of her head, and pull the trigger? For God's sake, the fireworks would even have masked the sound of the shots. Jocelyn couldn't have set it up better herself.

And where was she now? Collecting the money from wherever she'd hidden it, in preparation for leaving town? Or was she finding some horrible new way to do damage? The note she'd left at my mother's building frightened me—who knew what she might do to carry out that threat?

With that in mind, I dialed Susan's number on my cell phone. When she didn't answer after four rings, I called my mother's number.

"Hello? Who is this?" It wasn't Susan's voice, it was my mother's, and she sounded unsteady, frightened.

I spoke as quietly as I could and kept an eye on the front door. "Mom, could you put Rachel on?"

"John! My God, are you okay? Are you safe?"

"Yes, I'm fine—what's wrong?"

"Oh, my God, I was so worried about you, when Rachel said that woman was threatening to kill you—"

"She's threatening all of us," I said. "We all have to be careful. That's why I asked Rachel to stay with you."

"But she called!"

"Who called? What are you talking about?"

"She called," my mother said again. "Just a little while ago. She told Rachel she was going to kill you—"

"Jocelyn called?"

"I didn't talk to her, Rachel did. She said it was the same woman who left the note. John, she told Rachel she had a knife to your throat and was going to kill you."

"Well, it wasn't true. I'm fine. Can you just put Rachel on the phone, please?"

"She's not here," my mother said. "She went to find you. She tried to call you first, but there was no answer."

My blood went cold. The call that had come in while I was being mugged. That had been Susan. And when I hadn't answered—

"Mom, please think carefully, did Rachel say where she was going?"

"Yes, yes, I have it here. Hold on." I heard papers rustling. I wanted to scream. "She wrote it down. She said she was going to Corlears Hook Park, to the bandstand. She said I should call the police if I didn't hear from her in an hour. It hasn't been an hour yet. Should I call them?"

"Yes," I said.

Chapter 26

The bandstand at Corlears Hook Park was built in the Depression and abandoned some time in the seventies. God only knows why it's still standing. Before Stonewall, before AIDS, and before AOL chatrooms, it used to be a popular cruising spot for East Village men looking to hook up. Now it was nothing, a decrepit pile behind a chain link fence that offered some crude shelter to the homeless during a rainstorm and convenient shadows for drug dealers to hide in at noon. But the truth was you didn't even see that many homeless or drug dealers any more—even they didn't feel safe there.

I climbed down the fire escape as quickly as I could without breaking my neck, then ran all out down to Houston Street. I dropped the knife in the first garbage can I passed. I couldn't afford to have the police find it on me when they arrived. I cut across Delancey, under the Williamsburg bridge, and over to Grand Street. These were long blocks, and I was badly out of breath by the time I rounded Cherry, but I kept going. My heart wasn't beating any more, it was exploding, twice per second, against the inside of my ribs. My throat was raw from the freezing air I was taking in and my legs were burning like I'd just climbed ten flights of stairs. But I couldn't stop, and I couldn't slow down. I hadn't asked my mother how long ago Susan had left—all I knew was that it hadn't been an hour yet. But a lot can go wrong in less than an hour. I pictured Jocelyn standing behind Miranda, aiming a gun at the back of her head, pulling back gently on the trigger. A lot can go wrong in less than a second.

The park was empty. Wire fences surrounded a pair of dirt baseball diamonds. Basketball hoops with no nets stood on either end of a concrete square. In the distance, the bandstand rose behind a screen of trees, their dead branches obscuring whatever might have been going on there. But when I passed them, there was nothing to see. The bandstand was as empty as the rest of the park. I found a hole in the fence that was supposed to block

access to it, and raced up to the structure. There was a
pair of bathrooms on one side, but they'd been locked
tight for years. I went around to the back, where a few
metal doors led to storage closets or God knows what,
but they were locked, too, or anyway wedged shut. The
whole thing was covered with ancient graffiti and surrounded by broken bottle glass, crushed beer cans, and
the droppings of the countless birds and rats that found
shelter there. There was nothing else—no sign of Susan,
none of Jocelyn, nothing.

I took out my cell phone again. It was futile, but I
speed-dialed Susan's number. Maybe she'd answer,
maybe she was safe after all, maybe Jocelyn hadn't found
her yet or Susan had managed to elude her. The phone
started to ring.

And offset by a half second or so, I heard the sound of
Ravel's *Bolero* beeping faintly, not in my ear, but from the
back of the bandstand.

I followed the sound to one of the doors in the rear, a
rusted metal door with no knob even, just a round hole
where you'd expect the doorknob to be. From behind it,
muffled but distinct, came the sound of Susan's cell
phone. Then the beeping stopped, and in my ear I heard
Susan's voice as her voicemail picked up: "Hi, I'm not
available right now—"

I slammed the phone shut, stuck two fingers through
the hole in the door, and pulled as hard as I could. It
didn't budge. "Susan," I shouted. There was no response.
"Help me get this open. Come on!" She had to be in
there. Unless it was just her phone, thrown there by
Jocelyn so Susan couldn't use it, but that didn't make any
sense—why would she go to the trouble of opening one
of these old doors just to get rid of a phone? I yanked
harder. I planted my foot against the wall for leverage

and pulled till it felt like my arms were tearing apart at the joints. The door started moving, slowly, a millimeter at a time. I pulled again, and again, and the metal groaned as the door scraped open an inch. I couldn't see inside. But now I had leverage. I wrapped my hands around the edge of the door and dragged it open. Half a foot. A foot. Two feet.

It was a narrow utility closet with a stripped circuit breaker box on the back wall. Susan was huddled on the ground in a heap. She wasn't moving. I touched the side of her face. It was cold.

I gently pulled her out of the closet and laid her on the ground. She was wearing the same sweater she'd had on the first night we'd talked at Keegan's, only it wasn't the color of ginger ale any more. The front was soaked through with blood.

In the distance, I heard sirens approaching, but that wasn't good enough. I thumbed 911 into my phone. "Send an ambulance to Corlears Hook Park," I said when the operator answered, "and hurry. A woman's been hurt, badly."

I tried to take her pulse. I couldn't feel it.

The waiting area at Bellevue's emergency room was packed. One boy with what looked like a broken arm was howling while his mother tried alternately to calm him down and get the attention of the triage nurse. But a broken arm could wait. There were head wounds, there were infectious diseases. This was one of the largest trauma centers in the world, but also one of the busiest, and there was never enough staff to go around.

But Susan was inside. Even at Bellevue, a chest wound like hers took priority. The ambulance had arrived in less than five minutes and had torn up First Avenue with its siren blaring, dodging around cars and pedestrians to shave seconds off our arrival time. Even so, I knew it might not have been enough. They said she'd lost a lot of blood—as though that wasn't obvious. They told me she was in critical condition. When I asked if she'd make it, they'd shrugged. EMTs had no time for politeness.

"She's got a chance," one of them had said. I'd been clinging to that ever since.

The cops had followed us to the hospital, adding their siren to the mix. They'd waited while I got her admitted, waited some more while I filled out paperwork as best I could. Last name: Feuer. First name: Susan. Home address? Home phone? Social security number? I left it all blank. Medical insurance provider? All I could do was hand over my credit card and hope I wasn't close to my limit.

They waited while I called Leo from a payphone and told him where I was and what had happened. They stood next to me and listened, but they waited.

Then they were done waiting. They steered me through the triage station to an empty administrative office just past the ER. Both were uniformed cops from the Seventh Precinct. One was about my height but twice my weight, with a round face and a thick moustache and a patch on his chest that said "Conroy." The other's patch said "Gianakouros" and belonged to a veteran with hair the color of old curtains and deep grooves creasing his face. He was the one who had me by the arm and he took the lead in questioning me.

"Your name?"

"John Blake."

"And the victim's name?"

"Susan Feuer. F-E-U-E-R."

"What's your relationship to the victim?"

"She's a friend. And we've been working together recently."

"What do you do, Mr. Blake?"

I took out my license and showed it to him. He handed it over his shoulder to Conroy, who jotted down the license number on a spiral-bound pad. "I work for Leo Hauser. He used to be at Midtown South. He has a small agency now—just the two of us, basically."

"And Feuer works with you?"

"No. She's just been helping me with one case I'm working on. Just as a favor."

"Some favor," Conroy said. He handed my license back.

"You want to tell us what happened?" Gianakouros said.

How to answer that? I wanted to, but this was not a story I could tell quickly. Where did it even start? When Susan began making calls for me, or before that when I first saw her dancing at the Sin Factory, or before that, when I opened the paper and saw Miranda's face staring out at me, all innocence and accusation? Or ten years earlier, when I'd seen Miranda last, when I'd sent her off on a boomerang voyage from New York to New Mexico and back again, from possibility to disaster and from life to death? I'd have to explain an awful lot if I wanted them to understand what had happened.

And I wouldn't mind explaining—but right now I couldn't afford the time. Jocelyn was still in town, but for how long? She was packed and ready to go. She'd just needed to sew up some loose ends, like the troublemaker who was calling all the strip clubs she'd ever worked at and trying to track her down. I'd set Susan on Jocelyn's trail, and somehow it had gotten back to her. Was it any wonder that Jocelyn had decided to eliminate Susan before leaving the city?

Now, Jocelyn probably just needed to pick up the money from wherever she'd stashed it and then she'd vanish forever. One of the country's best agencies hadn't been able to find her the last time she'd gone on the road, and back then she hadn't had a half million dollars to help her hide.

"We're looking for a missing woman named Jocelyn Mastaduno," I said. "Her parents haven't heard from her in six years and they want to know what happened to her. Susan was helping me make some calls to track her down."

"What was she doing in the park?"

"I don't know," I said.

"How did you know she was there?"

"Susan was staying with my mother. She told her she was going to the park, and my mother mentioned it to me."

"So you went there."

"I was worried," I said. "I didn't understand why she'd gone there, and the park can be dangerous at night."

Conroy spoke up. "Any idea who might have done this?"

"None," I said.

"What about this woman you're looking for, Mastaduno?"

"It's possible. I just don't know."

"How close are you to finding her?"

Pretty close, I thought—if I can get out of here. I fought to keep my voice calm. "I can't say. We're not the first agency to work on it. The last one took a year and never found her."

"Maybe you're closer than they were."

"Maybe," I said.

"If Miss Feuer could tell us who she was meeting in the park, we might have something," Gianakouros said. "But she's not going to be doing much talking any time soon. Not with multiple stab wounds in her chest."

No, not soon. Maybe not ever.

"We're going to canvass the area for witnesses tonight, people in the neighborhood, anyone who might have seen it happen. But we're also going to need to talk to you some more."

"And your mother," Conroy said.

"That's right, your mother, and Mastaduno's parents, and anyone else you can think of who might know something about this. We're going to need any information you have."

"That's fine," I said. "But can we do it in the morning? I can't think straight now." They looked at each other. "I'm sorry, it's just too much. I'm a wreck." I held my hands up. They were trembling, and it wasn't an act. "First thing in the morning, nine A.M., I'll be there. I promise, I'll help any way I can. I'm just not up to it now."

"Eight A.M.," Gianakouros said. "Wreck or no wreck. We need you."

"Thank you," I said.

Conroy's voice softened. "You want us to ask the doctor if you can look in on her?" he said. "Maybe she's out of surgery."

I shook my head. "Five stab wounds to the chest, there's only one way she'd be out of surgery this soon. So I hope to God she isn't."

Why hadn't I told them? It would have been simple. I had Jocelyn's address. They could have gone right now and arrested her, or if she wasn't there, they could have staked the apartment out and waited for her to arrive. They could at least have taken the luggage cart in as evidence, gotten fingerprints and blood from it, tied Lenz's murder to Miranda's, gotten me off the hook in Queens, begun the process of tracking her down—something. But I hadn't done it.

It would have been the right thing to do—I knew that. But the time was past for doing the right thing. It had passed when Jocelyn lured Susan down to the park and sank a blade five times into her chest. The person who did that, the person who murdered an innocent woman and left her body on a strip club roof, the person who shot Wayne Lenz in cold blood and left me to take the fall, a person who could do those things didn't deserve to be arrested and prosecuted and defended and maybe sent to jail or maybe not, depending on how sympathetic a jury she found. What she deserved, the police and the courts weren't the ones to deliver.

I waited till I was well away from the hospital and confident that neither Conroy nor Gianakouros was following me. I dialed the number and waited while it rang. When the hoarse voice said "Yes?" I hesitated for a second. There would be no turning back.

"Yes?" he said again.

"I found her," I said. "And I'll give her to you, on one condition."

"What's that, Mr. Blake?" Murco said.

"I want her to suffer," I said.

Chapter 27

"You surprise me," he said.

I kept walking, retracing the ambulance's path, heading back toward Avenue D. "She attacked a friend of mine," I said. "This friend may not survive."

"I see. And now my methods don't seem so . . . inappropriate?" he said. "Never mind, you don't have to answer that. Tell me, Mr. Blake, does she still have my money?"

"It's not in her apartment, or if it is, she's hidden it well. But I'm sure she knows where it is, and I'm sure you'll be able to get it out of her."

"You make it sound so simple," he said softly. "Sometimes it can be like pulling teeth."

Did he think he was being funny? I felt my stomach twist. I forced myself to remember Susan's bloody body in my arms and Miranda lying on the roof at midnight, half her face blown away by a pair of hollow-point bullets.

I gave him the address. "How soon can you get here?"

"It takes me forty-five minutes to get into the city," he said.

"How about your son?"

"He'll meet me there."

"Well, I'm not waiting. I'm not taking a chance that she gets away while you're driving in."

"It almost sounds like you want her worse than I do," he said.

"You can get back what she took from you," I said. "I can't."

*

I thought about stopping by the office on the way down-town, but it would take too long to cross to the West Side and anyway, what was the point? Maybe if we'd had another gun—but the only guns we owned were now in the possession, respectively, of Little Murco Khacha-durian and the 109th Precinct in Queens.

The blocks went by, empty and dark. I felt the cold on my face, but inside my jacket I was sweating. What if Jocelyn was already gone by the time I got there? She'd presumably headed home while I was running to the park, and since then she'd had almost two hours to grab her things and take off. Of course, if taking off had been her plan, she could have done it as soon as she took the luggage cart with the money out of Lenz's apartment. She hadn't, and there had to be a reason, though I couldn't imagine what it was.

It wasn't the only point that bothered me. There was the luggage cart itself, the one that first turned up in Lenz's hands in the hallway outside Miranda's apartment on the afternoon of the murder. It made sense as long as you assumed that Miranda had the money in her apart-ment and that Lenz had needed a way to get it out—but if Jocelyn and Lenz had the money all along, what the hell did he need to take a luggage cart to Miranda's apart-ment for? The only thing Lenz had needed to do in her apartment was plant the torn paper band that would tie her to the burglary. You didn't need a piece of luggage to carry that.

And what about that paper band? Could the police really have missed it lying behind the dresser? Sure, it was possible, cops missed things, especially if they didn't look very hard—but Jocelyn and Lenz couldn't have *counted* on their missing it. And the last thing they would have wanted was to run the risk of getting the police more interested in what was otherwise a relatively routine homicide. Yet that's exactly the effect that finding a band from a stack of hundred dollar bills would have had. Murco was the one who was supposed to find the band and make the connection, not the police—which meant that the right time for Lenz to plant it would have been after the murder, after the cops had come and gone, not before. But in that case, what was Lenz doing in Miranda's apartment before the murder?

I'd gone over these questions in my head countless times over the past few days, and the answers just didn't get any clearer.

I crossed Fourteenth Street and passed an empty cab stopped at a red light. Did I have enough cash? I dug into my pocket, decided I did, and got in. This would give me a chance to catch my breath, at least, and get me past any encounters I might otherwise have in Alphabet City. Barring traffic, it would also get me there faster. "Avenue D and Fifth," I said. We roared off as the light changed.

I tried not to think about what Murco would do when he got here. Jocelyn needed to be stopped, and more than that she needed to be punished, and Murco would see to both—but I didn't want to think about it too closely.

What I thought about instead was what I would do. The sensible part of my brain was telling me to watch from the street, maybe from the doorway of one of the projects across the avenue, to follow her if she came out, but otherwise to stay where I was and not get involved. When Murco showed up, I should point the apartment out to him and then walk away.

But I had too many questions, too many things I needed to understand. I needed to face her, to look Jocelyn in the eye, to hear from her own mouth what had happened, how she could have killed someone we'd both loved.

I stopped the cab a half block early, paid and walked the rest of the way. The fire escape ladder was still down, and one of the windows in Jocelyn's apartment was still dark. But the other window, the kitchen window, was brightly lit. My heart was pounding. There was no one coming from either direction. I took hold of the ladder, pulled myself silently up to the first rung, and started to climb.

I didn't have the knife with me this time, but I also hadn't closed the bedroom window all the way on my way out. There was enough room for me to get my fingertips under it and slowly raise it. The room was dark, but the light from outside was sufficient to show that the bed was still empty, the comforter pushed to one side exactly as I had left it. I stepped inside and quietly pulled the window closed. Through the bedroom door I could hear the sound of the television going in the living room. I couldn't make out the words, but it seemed to be a news program, maybe CNN or NY1. Footsteps crossed from the living room to the kitchen. A glass was set down on the countertop, or maybe in the sink. Then I heard water running.

The TV on and water running—I wasn't likely to have a better chance than that to open the door unnoticed. So I turned the knob carefully and drew the door back. I followed the hallway past the bathroom to the living room. The kitchen was on my right, a pair of narrow French doors flung open on either side. I crept up to the one closer to me.

She was at the sink, with her back to me. She was wearing black jeans and black canvas sneakers and a hooded grey sweatshirt with the hood draped down between her shoulders. A plate and a fork were set out to dry on a rubber tray next to the sink, and from the way her arms were moving, it looked like she was working on the glass.

"Don't move, Jocelyn," I said. "My name is John Blake, and I'm—"

I heard the glass slip and smash in the bottom of the sink. One of her hands leaped to her chest. "Jesus, you scared me," she said, turning around. "You shouldn't do that, John. Sneaking up on me like that, after all this time."

And suddenly I was back where it all began, staring in blank confusion at a picture from the past. Because it wasn't Jocelyn.

It was Miranda.

Chapter 28

"How's your head?" Miranda said. "Sorry I had to hit you so hard, but you really didn't give me any choice. It was either that or kill you, and I really didn't want to kill you." She was holding a steak knife in one hand and had picked up a piece of the broken glass in the other, but when she looked at my hands and saw that they were empty, she dropped both on the rubber tray and came forward. "Don't need those, I guess. You're not going to hurt me, are you? Poor, sweet John. I can still hear you telling Wayne how all you wanted was for me to be alive again. It touched me. Seriously."

She was a foot away from me. She put a hand up to my

face, touched my cheek. I felt her fingertips against my skin as though from a mile away. She said, "You're going to have to talk to me, sweetie. This isn't going to work otherwise."

Like one of those optical illusions where first the cubes seem to be pointing in one direction and then suddenly they're pointing in the other, and you can't imagine how they could ever have looked like they weren't.

"Miranda—" The words wouldn't come. Everything was wrong. If Miranda was here, was alive, then who . . . ? "Jocelyn. You killed Jocelyn."

She shrugged. "I'd be dead now if I hadn't."

"And Lenz. You killed them both."

"Look, if we're going to have this conversation, let's sit down." I didn't move. "You want to stand? Fine, John, we'll stand." She leaned against the refrigerator, crossed her arms over her chest.

"How could you do it?"

"Do you mean how could I or how did I? Are you disgusted with me, or just confused?"

"Both," I said.

"It's not so hard, baby. Really, it isn't. You do what you have to do to get by. But you've learned that, too, haven't you?"

"What happened to you?" I said, in a small voice.

"To me? What about you? All these years, I always pictured you down at NYU thinking great thoughts, reading—I don't know, ancient Greek history or something. I figured you'd be a professor, or maybe a scientist—or, or, I don't know, you'd go into politics, I'd turn on the news and there you'd be, running for mayor of New York. I'll tell you, it made it easier when I was dancing in every cheap dive across the South. At least one of us was doing better, you know? I certainly didn't picture you doing this. Working with drug dealers, breaking into people's apartments. Chasing after strippers with blood on their hands."

"You were going to be a doctor," I said.

"I was going to be a lot of things." She came forward again, gently pushed me out of the doorway so she could step through. "At least let me turn off the TV."

I caught her arm as she passed, stepped out into the living room with her. "What," she said, "you don't trust me? I'm not going to do anything." She kept her hands high as she went to the couch, picked up the remote control, and turned the TV off. "See?" She sat down. "Now you."

I sat across from her. It was beyond comprehension. That she was here at all, that I was, that we were sitting across from each other like old friends catching up after years apart, all while Susan lay in the hospital, clinging to life, and Jocelyn lay in the morgue, half her face blown away, deliberately misidentified to the police by Lenz. On one level, it all finally made sense—the pieces fit. But on another, it made no sense at all.

"It was you dancing at the Wildman," I said. "Not Jocelyn. Danny Matin said it was you and so did the bartender, and it wasn't because she looked like you, it was because it *was* you."

"Yeah, it was me." She lit a cigarette, held the pack out to me, dropped it on the coffee table when I didn't react. "I'm not proud of what I did there, but I did it."

"But why did you use her name?"

"I couldn't use mine—not to set up a robbery. And they won't hire you in a strip club these days without seeing ID. I had an old ID of Jocelyn's from when we were dancing together. The picture was close enough."

Close enough. And when the burglars she'd recruited

were caught and tortured and killed, and she'd needed someone to die in her place on the roof of the Sin Factory, Jocelyn had been close enough for that, too. Jocelyn, who was still in love with her, and who came running, bringing flowers no less, when Miranda had called her out of the blue offering a reconciliation. I thought about the message on the answering machine—Miranda hadn't set herself up accidentally, she'd set Jocelyn up, very deliberately.

"How did you get Lenz to go along with it?" I asked.

"What choice did he have? He's the one who'd told me about the buy in the first place. He shouldn't have, but the man couldn't keep his mouth shut. He just had to brag. And thank goodness. If he hadn't, I'd have been working at that dive for nothing, not to mention fucking him for nothing." She put on an expression of mock sympathy. "I'm sorry, sweetie. You didn't think I'd been saving myself for you, did you?"

"Hardly," I said.

"I remember the day he came home from that bar and said Khachadurian's son had been in and had told everyone they'd caught the men who'd robbed his father. Wayne was so happy. He told me, 'Those sons of bitches got what they deserved.' " She took a long drag on the cigarette. "You know what Khachadurian did to them?"

"Yes," I said, "I know what he did."

"Well, I had to give Wayne the bad news. I told him, 'If we don't do something and fast, you and I are going to be in the same boat as those sons of bitches, because I'm the one who told them about the deal, and you're the one who told me.' I thought he was going to have a heart attack, drop dead right there."

She waited for me to say something, but I didn't know what to say.

"Wayne had two choices," she went on. "He could go to Khachadurian, explain what had happened, and beg for mercy, in which case the best he could hope for was that maybe they'd just kill him instead of cutting out his eyes first, or he could agree to help me. And let's not forget that if he helped me, he also got half the money. And he got me. All he had to do was identify her body as mine and then let me stay at his apartment until the heat died down."

That wasn't quite true. He could identify Jocelyn's body as Miranda's, but the word of a two-time convict might not be enough for the police. And while expanding shells pumped into the back of a person's head could do a lot to interfere with either a visual or a dental identification, they couldn't change one person's DNA into another's. If the police picked up anything at Miranda's apartment for a comparison, Miranda needed to know they'd get trace amounts of Jocelyn's hair and skin, not hers. Even a drop-out pre-med would know that.

Meanwhile, Miranda needed to have clothing to wear while she was in hiding, but she couldn't empty her apartment without making the police suspicious. Fortunately, there was a simple solution to both problems: the afternoon of the murder, Miranda could take Jocelyn out on the town, and while they were away from both apartments, Lenz could come down to Avenue D, fill a big, rolling suitcase with Jocelyn's clothing, hairbrush, toothbrush, and so forth, and then go to Miranda's apartment and swap the contents of the suitcase for the things Miranda needed. That's how Jocelyn's baseball cap had ended up hanging on the inside of Miranda's door. The clothing in Miranda's dresser had been Jocelyn's, too, or at least the things on the top of each drawer had been. The luggage cart had never had money in it—just Jocelyn's things on the way in and Miranda's on the way out.

And the paper band behind the dresser? Maybe it really had fallen there by accident, and just gone unnoticed by everyone until Little Murco turned it up.

"You're lucky," I said. "Once everyone thought you were dead, it would have been simple for Lenz to kill you for real and just keep all the money for himself."

"Sure," she said, "if he'd known where the money was."

"How could you keep it hidden while you were staying at his apartment?"

"Oh, John, come on, I'm not that stupid," she said. "I didn't keep it at the apartment. I put it in a safe deposit box. Or I should say Jessie Masters did, since that's who the bank thought it was renting to."

And that explained why she hadn't left the city after killing Lenz—the murder had taken place on Friday night, and a bank wouldn't let her get into her safe deposit box until Monday morning. Yes, all the pieces fit now. It had all been constructed so carefully, right from the start. I thought back to what Susan had said that first night at the Derby about how Miranda had told her in the dressing room that she was afraid that Murco was going to kill her. It was a perfect way to set the stage for her apparent death the next day. There might be some dispute later about who'd killed Miranda, but not about whether it had actually been Miranda who'd died. She'd put it all together masterfully.

"You really thought of every angle."

"A girl's got to take care of herself," she said. "Jocelyn taught me that."

A girl's got to take care of herself—even if doing so meant killing. It had meant killing Lenz when it had looked like he might talk. It had meant killing Susan, or trying to, presumably because she was making too many calls to too many people, asking too many questions, getting too close. And now did it mean killing me? I imagined it had to, despite what she'd said about not wanting to.

"What happens now?" I said.

"You tell me, baby," she said. "I'm not going to go to jail. Not after everything I've been through. And I'm certainly not going to let you hand me over to Khachadurian. I don't want to kill you, John, I swear to God I don't, but it's kind of up to you, isn't it?"

She reached between the cushions of the couch and came up with a knife. It was a simple steak knife, the same sort as the one she'd left by the sink, probably the same sort she'd used on Susan. Maybe the same one, washed clean and ready for another use. She wasn't holding it in a threatening manner, not yet, but she was pointing it in my general direction. Her eyes had a question in them. I stood up.

"Don't," I said. "Don't pretend you're giving me a choice. Do me that one favor, Miranda. Don't treat me like you treated the others. I'm sure you told them it was up to them, too, that as long as they worked with you, you'd be on their side. That you loved them. It lasted just as long as you needed them, and then when you didn't any more, when it was more convenient to you for them to be dead, all the sweet talk went out the window."

"It's not the same," she said. "It's not. Wayne Lenz was a disgusting man. It made me sick to touch him. And you know what Jocelyn did to me? After nine years, after I followed her across the whole goddamn country, after I gave up everything for her, she takes one look at this . . . at this . . . *woman*, and I don't matter any more. After *nine years*, John. You can't imagine what it's like." She stood up and came toward me. The knife was between us. "I've never had anyone, John, not since you. That's the truth. No one I could trust." I saw tears forming in her eyes. "You were always good to me. If you said you'd leave me alone, if you swore that you wouldn't tell anyone, I know you'd keep your word. You've changed, but you haven't changed that much."

Now the point of the knife pressed against my shirt, and through my shirt, against my chest. "But I have to know. I can't let you out of here otherwise. I can't."

I saw her in front of me, holding the knife to my chest, but I also saw her as she had been at age eighteen. Where along the way had Miranda turned into the person she was today? How had it happened? Was there any trace of my Miranda still in there somewhere? Or was there only the murderer, the betrayer, the woman who deserved the sort of punishment I'd imagined in the cab on the way downtown? I wanted to believe there was more. I wanted to desperately.

I reached out, touched her wrist gently. "You can put the knife away," I said. "I won't hurt you, Miranda. I could never hurt you."

"Swear it," she said.

"I swear."

"On your life. On your mother's life."

"I swear," I said. "On everything I love, on everything I care about. On *your* life, Miranda. I swear. Now put the knife away."

"I want to believe you," she said.

"I may be many things, Miranda, but I'm not a liar. Put the knife away."

"Just give me a few days," she said. "I'm realistic, I'm not asking for forever. But don't tell anyone for a week, okay? I can get far away in a week."

"Okay," I said. "One week."

The knife lowered. It was by her side, and then her fingers opened and it dropped to the floor. She was crying freely now, tears streaming down her cheeks. I took her in my arms and realized that I was crying, too, for her, for both of us. How had we ended up here, in a filthy tenement with a knife on the floor between us, she a killer and I—and I—

I stroked her hair back behind her ear with a thumb, and tried not to think about anything, tried only to feel her in my arms, to burn this fragile instant into my memory.

I let her go. I lifted her chin and pressed my lips against her forehead. "Goodbye, Miranda."

"One week," she said.

"One week," I said. "I promise."

She stood at the door as I went downstairs. At the first turn of the stairway, I looked back and saw her there, leaning against the door, framed in the light. If this was going to be the last image I ever had of her, despite everything, I was grateful for it. I've never hated myself as much as I did at that moment.

I turned back and kept going down.

They were waiting on the sidewalk when I opened the building's front door. They were wearing heavy overcoats and leather gloves and dark fur hats with flaps to cover their ears. The father was patting his hands together impatiently, while the son stood absolutely still, looking at me over his father's head.

"Where were you," Murco said. "We've been here ten minutes. We were starting to think you'd double-crossed us."

"She's upstairs," I said.

Chapter 29

Leo stood beside me at the foot of the hospital bed. Susan looked terrible—pale, drawn, in pain. But she was alive. The doctors had told us that she'd regained consciousness briefly, but now she was asleep, the thin sheet over her bandages hardly rising and falling at all with her shallow breaths.

Leo tugged on my sleeve and I followed him out into the waiting room. "You're going to have to tell them everything," he said, speaking quietly.

"Leo, I need you to take care of this for me. I've never asked for anything like this before, but I'm asking now."

"There are three precincts involved, Johnny. I can't just wave a wand and make it go away."

"Do you think I should go to Murco?" I said.

"Murco will be lucky to keep himself out of jail," Leo said. "If what you're telling me is true."

"I wish it weren't."

"Let's not forget," he said, "that I told you so."

"Yes, you did. So did she." *Stop looking for me*, she'd written, *or you'll be sorry*. I hadn't, and I was.

I was trying very hard not to think about what Murco had done to her in the hours since I'd walked out of her building. I tried to think instead about Susan and Jocelyn and even Lenz and the two burglars, all the lives she'd ruined. But all I could see was her face at the door, tears in her eyes, begging me to give her a week's head start and trusting me when I said I would. She'd turned into something unspeakable in the ten years since we'd known each other—but was what I'd turned into so much better?

"It's almost eight," Leo said. "You'd better go."

I zipped up, went out, hailed a cab. "Pitt Street," I said.

They kept me there all day. I told the story, and then I told it again, and I kept telling it until they stopped asking me to. Different cops came and went. I saw Kirsch stick his head in once, and once I thought I saw Lyons from Queens through an open door, but mostly it was Frank Gianakouros and me, questions and answers, back-to-back sessions with no bathroom breaks and only coffee to keep me going. They were trying to wear me down till the truth came out. What they didn't realize was that I was giving them the truth. Maybe not the whole truth, but certainly the truth.

Jocelyn had never had her prints taken and neither had Miranda—but now that they knew it mattered, they'd take a closer look at what was left of Jocelyn's teeth, do a DNA match on whatever they could turn up in the apartment on Avenue D, match any prints from Avenue D to the partials they said they'd found on Leo's gun. I'd given them the videotape, which Leo had brought from the office, along with a sheet of phone numbers: Daniel Mastaduno, Bill Battles, Danny Matin. I'd told them about Roy and Keegan and what I knew about Lenz. I'd basically given them everything I had.

All I hadn't done was tell them about the role Murco had played at the beginning and end of the affair. The burglary, sure—there was no way to tell the story without that. But what had happened to the burglars? I had no idea. How much had they stolen from Murco? I couldn't speculate. And what had happened to the money? Not for me to say. All I knew was that Miranda had conspired with Lenz to rob their mutual employer and that they'd killed Jocelyn to cover their tracks. Then Miranda had killed Lenz to cover hers, and had tried to kill Susan for much the same reason. And what had happened to Miranda? I didn't know. The apartment was empty when I got there.

They left me sitting in the interrogation room from five o'clock on, and it was seven before the door opened again. When it did, Leo came in with Gianakouros. Neither man looked happy. "You've got some good friends behind you," Gianakouros said.

"Don't make it sound like I'm pulling strings, Frank," Leo said. He turned to me. "They found the rest of the statue she hit you with in a trash can on Parsons Boulevard. That, and the luggage matches. It took a while, but the 109th is satisfied you're clean for Lenz's killing. And nobody's got any reason to hold you in connection with the attack on Susan. Right?"

Gianakouros nodded, reluctantly. "She backs up your story. Says it was Sugarman."

"Susan's awake?"

"On and off," Leo said.

"Can I see her?"

He looked at Gianakouros. "I've got no reason to hold you," Gianakouros said. "That's what I'm being told."

"Do you disagree?" Leo said.

"All I'm saying is, I hope I have half the clout you do when I've been off the force as long as you have."

"It's not clout, Frank. The boy didn't do anything."

The boy sat there and kept his mouth shut. Gianakouros wrestled with it for a minute. "He obstructed a police investigation. He could have told us all this last night."

"He was in shock," Leo said. "A woman he knows had just been stabbed practically to death. Anyway, he's telling you now."

"Sure, twelve hours later. Sugarman could be any-where by now."

"You're going to book him for that?"

"No," Gianakouros said. "But I don't have to like it." He turned to me. "Get out of here."

As badly as I needed it, I didn't even stop in the bath-room on the way out.

We stopped at a Burger Heaven instead. Leo ordered a cheese danish at the counter and I found my way to the men's room. When I got back, he handed me half.

"Thanks, Leo," I said. "You really came through."

"It's just a fucking cheese danish."

"You know what I'm talking about."

"Yeah. Well. I'm all out of favors in the department now, so you'd better not get in any more scrapes."

"I don't plan to," I said.

"You didn't plan to this time."

"There's not going to be a next time," I said.

Visiting hours were ending as we came through the lobby, but the nurse on Susan's floor agreed to let us in for a few minutes.

Susan didn't look any better than she had in the morning, but now her eyes were open. She said some-thing. I couldn't hear it. I leaned close to her mouth.

"Thank you," she said. Her voice was a small whisper.

I found her hand under the sheet, gripped it tightly.

"Chest hurts like hell," she whispered.

"You'll be okay."

"Never dance again," she whispered. "Scars."

"You kidding? The fetish crowd will love it." A small smile.

"We should have known it was Miranda," she whispered. "Only person who would know . . . about your childhood apartment."

She was right, I realized: there was no way Jocelyn could have known to look for me at my mother's apartment or to leave a threatening letter for me there; even if she'd somehow followed me to the right building, she wouldn't have known what apartment I'd gone to or what my mother's name was. Miranda, of course, knew both. It was the sort of thing you always think of when it's too late to do any good.

"Don't worry about it," I said again.

"Police said," Susan whispered, then she had to stop and take another breath. It hurt to see her strain. ". . . Miranda got away."

"She didn't," I said.

I was exhausted, but still couldn't close my eyes without seeing Miranda. I didn't want to face her in my dreams. I'd have to eventually, but any excuse to put it off was welcome.

I called Daniel Mastaduno. He'd already heard from the police, but he still took it badly. What did I expect? It was his daughter, whom he loved, and no matter what he'd said, he'd never given up hope. Well, he could give up now.

I told him to call me later if he wanted to talk about it any more, ask any questions. He said, "No. Thank you, Mr. Blake. I don't want to know any more. I wish I didn't know this much. We were happy when we thought she was out there somewhere, living her life, and just didn't want to talk to us. We didn't know it, but we were."

The terrible thing was, I knew he was right. I'd set out to do some good, for him, for Jocelyn, for Miranda, and I'd brought nothing but pain to everyone. Susan was hooked up to tubes and could hardly speak. I was still aching and bruised. The only person I'd actually helped was Murco Khachadurian.

Well, it wasn't too late for one last attempt. I called Bill Battles, at home.

"John! Am I your one phone call?"

"I'm not in jail," I said.

"I thought I heard they were holding you."

"They were. They let me go."

"You didn't give them our file, did you?"

"It wasn't mine to give."

"Good, good. They'll probably subpoena it, but that's fine. We'll give it to them when we see a court order saying we have to."

"There's nothing in it, Bill. What difference does it make?"

"Matter of principle," he said. "You can't start caving in every time NYPD asks for something. They'll think they can walk all over you."

"Listen, Bill," I said, "you know how you're always saying you're looking for good people?"

"Sure—but John, I don't know, you're a little hot right now for a firm like ours . . . "

"Not me," I said. "There's a woman I used on this case. She's new to the business, but she's damn good at it. A real natural. She broke the case for me in three days, just working the phone. I was thinking Serner would be a great place for her to learn the ropes. Just phone work, though—not out on the street."

"Why don't you want her yourself?"

"A little firm like ours? You think Leo can afford another head?"

"What's her name?"

"Susan Feuer." I heard the scratch of a pencil against

paper. "She got hurt on the case. She's in the hospital now, recovering. But when she gets out—"

"I'll talk to her," he said. "No promises."

"Of course. I'm just telling you, she's great."

"We can always use someone great," he said. "When things quiet down, maybe we can even talk about you. Just not now, you understand."

"I don't want a new job, Bill," I said. "I'm not sure I even want the one I have."

Sleep came quickly, and at first it was the blank, dreamless sleep of the bone-tired. But somewhere along the way I had the impression of waking up. Only I wasn't in my apartment any more—I was in Miranda's, and not the one on Avenue D or the one on Fifteenth Street, but the one from our childhood. We were in bed together, side by side, and we were both young and hopeful and unscarred. But her hair smelled the way it had on Avenue D, and she felt in my arms as she had the last time I'd held her.

She unfolded a Rianon brochure, held it up so I could see the green lawns and pueblo-style buildings, and she pointed to a photo of the medical school campus. "I'm going to go the pre-med program for ophthalmology," she said, "but just for a couple of years. Then I'm going to drop out and drive across the country, working as a stripper with a girlfriend. She'll betray me, eventually, and I'll kill her, but not because of what she's done to me, just because she's handy. I'm pretty sure that's what I'm going to do. What about you?"

What about me.

"I'll hunt you down," I said, "not even knowing that's what I'm doing, and then when I find out, I'll hand you over to the man who kills you."

She snuggled closer. "At least tell me it'll be painless, sweetie."

"No," I said, "it will be horrible. For both of us."

"Why, John? Why do we have to end up that way?"

"We don't have to," I said. "But we will."

"And it's too late for us to change?" she said.

"For you it is," I said.

Chapter 30

I spread the paper out on the table, flattened it down with both hands, and we stared at the photos. They'd run the same shot of Miranda, only now a photo of Susan was next to it, and next to that, one of me. I'd ended up in the paper after all.

It was a longer story this time and got more prominent placement, filling page three and continuing on page seven. The headline said, "New Attack Leads to Breakthrough In Stripper Murder." I left my mother to read the rest of the article.

"I had no idea," she said when she finished. "Rachel seemed like such a nice girl. Susan, I suppose I should say."

"She is a nice girl," I said. "She just had a lousy job."

"And Miranda, too. How do these girls end up doing something like that?"

"How did I end up doing what I do?"

"That's completely different. You help people."

"That's what I used to think," I said.

"Do you really mean to give it up?"

I drank some more of her hazelnut coffee and thought about how much can change in a week. I nodded.

"Leo will be awfully disappointed."

I thought about it. He would be. I remembered him warning me to be careful when this whole thing started. *I'm too old to start again with some other kid.* And he was. But I just couldn't do it any more.

"He'll manage," I said.

"Well, you have to decide what's best for you, John. I just don't know, going back to school at your age . . . "

"I'm twenty-nine," I said. "I think I've got a few years left in me."

"What are you going to study? Poetry again?"

"I don't know yet. I just need to do something other than what I've been doing."

"Have you told Leo yet?" she asked

I shook my head. "You're the first."

Was it a good decision? I thought about it as I rode down in the elevator. Maybe not. I wasn't sure what I'd study, or what I'd do afterwards. In spite of what Miranda had said, I didn't see myself as a professor, and God knows I didn't have the stomach for politics. But there would be something for me, and whatever it was, it would more or less have to be a step up.

It was a sunny morning, but a cold one, the kind where the wind rushes through you, burning every pore. Outside my mother's building, a week's worth of accumulated trash was stacked for pick-up at the curb, most of it in heavy black plastic bags cinched with wire, but some of it just lying out in the open. There was an upended mattress and next to it a narrow bookcase. There were a few stacks of paperback books that looked like they'd been rummaged through. I saw the cardboard hatboxes from

Mrs. Knechtel's apartment and one of the framed posters, and that's when I realized what I was looking at. They must have finished cleaning her apartment out over the weekend. This was the accumulated stuff of a life, left out for any scavenger who saw something he liked and for the garbage trucks that would cart away the rest.

I walked past the pile, then stopped and came back. I'd only seen it out of the corner of my eye, sitting on top of a rolled-up carpet, half hidden behind one of the garbage bags. I wasn't even sure that I had seen it. It seemed impossible. But yes, there it was, still in its dusty, wretched cage, plastic beak and wire feet and all, looking much the same as it had ten years earlier when I'd left it on the rim of the sink in the garbage room. The decade hadn't left a mark on it. I stared at it, dumbfounded.

How . . . ? Mrs. Knechtel, I thought. Maybe she'd been the one who threw it out in the first place, and when she saw it again ten years later, sitting on the edge of the sink, she couldn't just leave it there. There is such a thing as loyalty, after all, and nostalgia for better times, and a sense of duty to the things of your past, even if they're not quite as beautiful as you remember.

We stared at each other for a good long while, the bird and I. I felt ridiculous picking it up off the carpet. I didn't care. I took it home.

More Great Books From
HARD CASE CRIME!

361

by DONALD E. WESTLAKE

THREE-TIME EDGAR® WINNER

The men in the tan-and-cream Chrysler destroyed Ray Kelly's life. Now it's Ray's turn.

Home Is the Sailor

by DAY KEENE

PULP LEGEND

Swede Nelson just wanted to meet a nice girl and settle down. So how did he find himself on the run, wanted for murder?

Kiss Her Goodbye

by ALLAN GUTHRIE

CWA DEBUT DAGGER NOMINEE

When his daughter is found dead, underworld enforcer Joe Hope will stop at nothing to find the man responsible.

To order, visit www.HardCaseCrime.com or call 1-800-481-9191 (10am to 9pm EST).
Each title just $6.99 ($8.99 in Canada), plus shipping and handling.